Heart OF A BOSS

3

A Memphis Love Story

D1275714

A NOVEL BY

JAMMIE JAYE

ACKNOWLEDGEMENTS

This book ends my first series as a published author. I would have never thought in a million years that is was the plan that God had in store for me. This time last year I was still finding myself. I had no idea what I really wanted in life. With a little encouragement from my husband, I made my dream of becoming a published author become my reality.

The first person that I have to give thanks to is God, because without him, none of this would be possible. He is the reason that I have made it this far. I also have to take a moment to say thanks husband for believing in me and pushing me when I felt like it was all too much to handle. I couldn't have done it without you by my side. Thanks to my friends and family for pushing me and listening to me complain about my books not being good enough.

Ms. Porscha Sterling, you are simply amazing, and thanks so much for believing in me and giving me a chance.

Thanks to each and every person who took time out of their day to download or purchase one of my books. To all of my test readers, you all are so awesome and greatly appreciated. Special thanks to Quiana Nicole for dealing with me changing my mind a million different times. Let me not forget my pen sisters, Chan, Vaneecia, Bianca, B. Love and Alexus for allowing me to bounce ideas off of them. You guys are the best. Y'all just don't know how much each and every one of you mean to me.

This series was so hard for me, because I felt like no matter what I wrote that it wouldn't be enough, but my readers have proven me wrong.

Last but not least, I have to thank my motivators, James and Jameia. You two are my reason. I do it all for you.

THANK YOU! THANK YOU!

Jammie Jaye

SHAYLA

My heart and mind have become so numb to pain. Every time things seem like that are getting good, something or someone gets in the way and fucks it all up. I just can't catch a fucking break. In most situations, I find a way to get over shit, but this one... I'm not too sure about this one. Losing my child was something that I never thought would happen. I won't get to see any of the important moments in her life. It's like within the blink of an eye, my baby was gone. I know that I should be blessed that I made it out safe, but I honestly would give my life for hers in a minute with no questions asked. I've seen people who have lost their child or children get up and keep moving like nothing has happened. Well, I can't do that. I feel like I want to die. All I want is my baby back.

I hadn't even realized that I was crying until I felt Kamery's arms wrap around me. His touch made me want to just melt. It was so warm and comforting. Who would have thought that in a year and half, we would be here? I thought that I would never love again.

"Baby, don't cry. I know it's hard, but we will get through this together. Just know that I'm going to paint the city red until I find who is responsible for this," he spoke. You could hear the anger in this voice. It made the hairs on the back of my neck stand up. I didn't reply, because no matter what he said or who he killed, it wouldn't bring Kayleigh back.

I stood there for a minute, just taking in the moment. After a while, I turned to face Kam, and my lady box instantly got wet. I backed up so that I could get a good look at him. My baby was looking good enough to eat. That shit made those tears I was crying dry up quick. He was only wearing some briefs and his favorite Gucci house shoes. I walked toward him and softly kissed him as he reached his hand under my oversized shirt and thumbed my clit. With no words spoken, I dropped to my knees and took his full length in my mouth.

"Damn, Shay. Fuck, I love you," he moaned as I made sure to wet every inch of his dick. I pulled his dick out of my mouth and sucked on the head until I felt his nut building up. Shortly after he released in my mouth, I made sure I left no evidence, if you know what I mean.

"Bend that ass over," he demanded. I did as I was told and bent my ass over. When he entered me, I had an instant orgasm. That didn't stop him, though. He kept punishing me. He was hitting my spot, back to back.

"Roll over. I want to look into those pretty ass eyes," he said as he pulled out of me. Again, I did as I was told and rolled over. He didn't even give me time to adjust myself before he was reentered me. It was like he knew just what to do each time that we made love. I came at least four times.

"Shit, baby. Slow down. I don't think that I can take it, baby. Please," I pleaded. My pleas went unheard, because he started going harder.

"Baby, you feel so good. You're going to make a nigga put another baby in yo' ass. Fuck, baby! Can daddy nut in that pussy?" he asked. I couldn't talk at this point. I was fighting to keep up with this strokes.

"I need to hear you, Shay. Tell daddy that he can nut in that pussy," he demanded.

"Daddy, please nut in this pussy," I begged. When I felt his dick contracting, my pussy came again. We just laid there, out of breath. Every time he wore my ass out.

"I love you, baby," he said, kissing me on the forehead.

"I love you too, baby. Now, get up and go and get our son I hear him crying," I said while laughing. He was the reason that KJ was so damn spoiled. As soon as he walked out the room, my phone rang. When I saw that it was my mother, I grabbed the phone and answered on speaker.

"Hey, ma."

"Hey, baby. How are my grandbabies doing?" my mother asked.

"They're good. SJ and Shan are out on the beach, and Kam just went to get KJ."

"Are you okay, Shay," my mother asked. I knew that question was coming sooner or later. I had been avoiding her for that reason. I knew it was messed up, but I didn't want to answer that. I hated lying to my mother. Anyone else, I didn't care about lying to. Even if I did lie, she would know it, so to save myself from getting cursed out, I just answered truthfully.

"No, ma. I'm not okay. I lost my daughter. Reagan still hasn't woken up, and Allynna is on life support. Jeano has a broken arm. Kaye has a broken arm. I just don't know what to do, ma. Why do people want to do harm to us. We haven't done anything to anyone," I cried. I was crying so hard that my head was starting to hurt. This was way too much for me. I would have never thought that my life would be this way.

"Well, baby... we just have to pray, and keep the faith. God will work it all out. I will be there sometime tomorrow. I'm flying commercial, so I should be okay. Have they said anything about the baby?" she asked.

"Not in the past couple of days. They did say that he is okay. They have run all kind of test on him and Reagan. I just need her to wake up, ma," I cried. I was so emotional, and I had no reason why. It seemed like every time that I turned around, I was crying, and that was not like me at all.

"Well, Shay... you cannot stress over stuff that you have no control over. You cannot change the things that have happened. You have to take life for what it is, and move forward," my mom explained. After we talked a little longer, I jumped in the shower so that I could go and see Reagan. I stayed in the shower until the water started to get cold. I just couldn't take life right now. Losing my child and not knowing if my best friend was going to make it was draining me. I did my best to hide the depression that I was falling into. I didn't know what I was going to do if I lost Rea. I was just letting the tears fall, hoping that all of my pain and worries would go down the drain with the water that was falling from my body.

"Things have to get better," was all that I managed to get out through the tears.

KAMERIN

Meanwhile, at the hospital…

"Baby, please wake up. Reagan… baby, I need you. I can't live without you and Kamden. I just need you here with me. I don't want to live this life without you by my side," I pleaded. I had been in this room, talking to Reagan nonstop since I was released from the hospital. The doctors told me that it was best if I talked to her. I just hoped that she could hear me.

"Baby, I thought that maybe we could just stay here. We don't have to go back to Memphis. We can just raise Kamden here. I've been looking at houses, and I saw a few that I know you will like, but I couldn't make any decision without you. As soon as you get out of here, we are going to look at them. Even if we just buy a vacation house here, that will be okay with me, too," I said as if I was going to get an answer. I know it sounded crazy for me to be sitting here talking to her, but I just needed my baby to get up and be okay.

I was sitting next to her, texting one of my guys in Memphis when my phone rang. It was an unknown number which made me hesitate answering it, but I decided that I would answer just to see who it was.

"Yeah?"

"Hey, Kaye," the unfamiliar voice said.

"Who is this?" I asked. Whoever it was had to be on some dumb shit, because they were calling private.

"This is Kelli," she said, and I instantly regretted answering the phone.

"What, Kelli? How can I help you?" I asked.

"I was just missing you, and hoping that I could see you."

"No, you can't see me. I have a wife, Kelli, so please don't call my phone again," I replied before ending that call. I didn't even give her a chance to reply. There was nothing that she needed to say to me.

Kelli was my girlfriend for a minute before I got with Reagan. She was cool until I caught the bitch stealing from me. What was crazy was that she wasn't stealing money. She was stealing product. She was going to the trap, telling the little homie that I sent her so that she could get high for free. I could support a shopping habit, but getting you high was out of the question.

Just as I was about to start back talking to Reagan, Jeano came in the door.

"What's good, big homie," I asked, shaking his hand.

"Shit… just need to talk to you about what's been going on in the city and check on Reagan," he mumbled.

"They said that the nigga that's out to get us is from Miami. He's supposed to be some kin to the nigga that Shay was fucking with. Kamin said that he was going to get with the Jaxon nigga's daddy and see what he could find out about the nigga," Jeano explained.

That all sounded kind of crazy if you ask me, because Jaxon's daddy was the one that lead us to him, so I know why he would be out for revenge. I think I know what could be going on, but I would have to deal with that shit another time. I was focused on getting my baby well.

We both fell silent for a while. I guess that like me, Jeano was calculating shit in this mind. After about twenty minutes, Jeano and I reverted our attention back to my wife. She was laying there with all these tubes and shit connected to her. Every time I looked at her, I wanted to cry. The only good thing was that all of the swelling in her face had finally gone down. She was starting to look like herself again. Every few minutes, I would rub her stomach and talk to my little man. If he didn't know anything, he would know the sound of his dad's voice.

I had been here for the past hour alone, talking to Reagan about random things as if she could reply. All I wanted was to see her big pretty eyes. I just needed her to wake up so that she could bring our son into the world. After talking for a while, I fell asleep holding her hand. When woke up after hearing my phone vibrate, I looked up, and those big brown eyes were staring straight at me. I was stuck in place until she tried moving and all of the machines started beeping. Before I could get up the nurses were rushing in. I wasn't one to cry, but at this moment, that was all I could do. My baby was okay as they pulled all of the tubes out. I called everyone to let them know that she was awake. As soon as they were done, I handed her a cup of water. She downed that damn water like she was dying of thirst.

The first thing that she did was grab her stomach.

"Is my baby okay?" she questioned with worry in her eyes.

"Yes… he's okay, baby," I confirmed. She looked so relieved and happy.

"Where is Shay? How are the babies?" she panicked. I didn't reply because I didn't want to lie to her. At that moment, I was saved by Kamery. He bypassed me and went straight to Reagan, kissing her all over the face. Had he been anyone other than my brother, I would have beat his ass.

"Nigga, stop kissing my wife," I playfully said. They all just looked at me and laughed. Those two were close and had always been, so it was to be expected.

"I'm glad you decided to wake up, because I want some green beans. Hurry up and get better. A nigga hungry," Kamery said to her, rubbing his stomach. That was all my brother thought about. He ate like a teenage boy.

"Nigga, my wife is not your damn maid or cook. She has to get well so that I can get in them guts," I playfully said. My baby just smiled, and that's all that I needed. Knowing that she was okay made my day. Now, all I needed was for her to bring my son into this world. That would complete me.

REAGAN

I had been struggling to open my eyes. No matter how hard I tried, I just couldn't. I could hear everyone talking to me. I just couldn't reply. I was so happy that I was able to. Just seeing my family made me feel so much better. The only thing that was worrying me was that Shay still was not here, and no one would tell me where she was.

Just as I was about to ask again, I started feeling pain in my lower back. I just shut my eyes until the pain subsided. I knew what meant, but I didn't want to ruin the moment that was playing out in front of me. Tears started to slowly run down my face. They weren't sad tears. They were actually happy tears. I had been through so much in the past year and a half. I was just happy that I survived it all. Just as I was about to get everyone's attention, Shayla walked in the room, and I forgot all about the pain that I was feeling.

"Hey, boo. How are you feeling?" she questioned. Just as I was about to reply, the pain shot through my back again. I knew that I couldn't hide the pain from her, so I just closed my eyes until it subsided.

"Y'all ass in here talking and ain't paying my damn sister no fucking attention. She's over here in labor, and y'all in your own fucking world," Shay fussed. Everyone ran to my side except Kaye. He was just standing there in a daze. As soon as we locked eyes, he ran out the room to get the nurse. At that point, it seemed that everything was happening so fast.

Before I knew it, I heard little cries and the tears started rolling. My baby was here and well. Kaye was so happy. He was smiling from ear to ear. I always thought that I would be tired after I gave birth, but for some reason, I was full of energy. More than likely, it was because I was in that coma for almost a month. After the doctors stitched me up, the nurse walked over and handed me Kamden RaSean Mareno. I couldn't be any happier. I had my husband, son, and family. That was all that I woman could ask for.

The doctors let the rest of the family in. They all had their focus on Kamden. I looked over at Kaye, and he was so happy. Outside of all the things that had happened, he was making due and smiling. That alone made me happy.

"You okay, baby?" he asked, rubbing my hand.

"Yes, I'm just so happy to be alive, baby. I'm just ready to get home and lay in a real bed," I whined. He just laughed.

After everyone played with the baby, they headed out. I had to stay one more day so that the doctor could keep watch over me since I had just gotten out of a coma. I watched Kaye play with Kamden for a while before I drifted off to sleep. When I woke up no one was there, except Jeano. He looked so disturbed and unhappy.

"You okay, Jeano? Where is Llynna?" I questioned. It had just hit me that everyone was here earlier except her.

"She's not doing well, and she lost the baby," Jeano cried. I think that was the first time that I had seen him emotional. He was always so strong. No matter how bad things got, he was always the one that was calm and mellow.

"Is it okay if I ask you something, Rea?"

"Yeah, go ahead," I said, adjusting myself in the uncomfortable hospital bed.

"Have you ever looked for your mother?" he asked. That kind of threw me for a loop because I had no idea why he would be asking me about my mother. Honestly, I had not thought about her in years.

"Not really. I have thought about it a few times over the years, but I didn't want to get disappointed. I really didn't care to know where she was in all honesty. I contacted my grandmother a few years back, and she told me that I had a brother. I had been meaning to have Kaye look into him, but over time, it came to mind that something would happen, and I would forget all about it. I would love to meet my brother though. As a matter of fact, can you find him for me?" I asked. I was hoping that the answer would be yes.

"You have already met your brother, Rea," Jeano mumbled. I was confused as to what he meant at this point. I had never seen my brother. The only way that I knew I had one was because of what my grandmother told me years ago when I first met her. She didn't even have a picture of him. She told me that my mother lost custody of him before I was born, and she couldn't find him. She didn't even know what his name was.

"What do you mean, Jeano?" I questioned. He was just sitting there, looking down at his hand like he was scared to tell me what he was talking about.

"I'm your brother," he confessed. I was at a loss for words. There is no way that he could be my brother. I knew people have told us that we favor, but that wouldn't make him my brother.

"You're going to have to give me more than that, Jeano," I fussed. I was starting to get irritated, because he was not explaining himself. He knew how much I hated that.

"As you know, I have been in foster care all of my life. Outside of you guys, I have no one. I wanted to find my family so that I could see if they wanted to build a relationship. I had Wiz to look for my mother. When he went to look for your mother after what you confessed on the plane, he informed us that she was my mother as well. She had you right after she had me. The state took me when she went to jail for prostitution, and then they took you because she was using while she was pregnant with you. She got you back shortly after she lost you. I found our grandmother, and she was the one that gave me your name. Neither of our fathers was listed," he explained.

I didn't know what to say. This was too much for me to take in. I couldn't believe my brother had been right here with me this whole time. I guess that's why we were so close and had the same last name.

He walked over to me and gave me the biggest hug ever. I was overjoyed. My whole life I felt like the only family that I had was Shay's family, and now, I have my own family. No matter how crazy things were, this had been the happiest day of my life, outside of the day that I married the love of my life. I couldn't wait to tell the family.

JEANO

I was so happy that Reagan was okay. I had known that she was my sister for the past month. I was just waiting on the right time to tell her. I was actually scared, because I thought that she wouldn't believe me. I was so happy that I got it off my chest.I just wished my baby was here to enjoy this moment with me. Allynna was still in ICU. They had been saying that she was doing better, but I didn't see it. Outside of that, she lost our baby.

I was so glad that Reagan had Kamden. We could finally go home and deal with all of these issues that we were having. After Reagan and I talked for a while, I headed back to down to ICU were Allynna was. I prayed that she got better so that I could go back to the "M" with her in tow. Leaving without her was not an option. I checked on her and headed to the house where everyone was. Before I could get out the door to my car, my phone was ringing.

"Hello?" I answered.

"You still at the hospital?" Kaye asked.

"Yeah, I was just about to leave,"

"Okay, don't. They are going to move Reagan and Allynna at the house. Pops said that he doesn't want anyone to try anything," Kay explained. As soon as he said that, I jetted to check on Reagan and Allynna. When I got to Reagan's room, she was feeding the baby, so I headed to check on Allynna. When I walked in the room, my heart dropped. She was gone. I called Kamin just to see if he had her moved, and when he said no, I could have died.

"They got her, Pops," I cried in the phone as I ran back to Reagan's side. I'd be damned if I let something happen to my sister. When I walked back in the room, she asked what was wrong.

"Somebody got Allynna," I cried. If I just would have moved faster I could have saved her. I knew she would never forgive me for letting this happen to her.

After about twenty minutes, the crew came to escort Reagan and I home. I felt relieved that she would be okay. Now, I had to find Allynna. Kam headed back to the hospital so that we could see what we could find out. There is no way that she just disappeared.

When we made to the hospital, I went to the floor that she was on to find the nurse that was over her room. The receptionist told me the nurse's name.

"Hey, I'm looking for Bethany Sringer," I asked one of the nurses that was sitting at the desk.

"I'm Bethany. How can I help you?" the nurse asked.

"Nah, you're not the nurse that was over my girlfriend. The nurse I'm looking for is short with red hair," I stated.

"What room was she in?" the nurse questioned.

"1435," I replied.

"There hasn't been a patient in that room at all, today."

"Ma'am I just left out of that room, so how are you going to tell me that no one was in that room? I'm not dumb," I stated.

"Sir, I am not saying that you are dumb. What is the patient's first name?" she questioned.

"Allynna. It's spelled A.L.L.Y.N.N.A."

"Sir, that patient is no longer here. She has been transferred, based on what the system is saying," she explained. This lady had to be losing her mind. I knew that I was just in the room with her, so there is no way that she could have been gone for three days. I was getting pissed, so I just snatched the iPad out of her hand to look for myself, and to my surprise, her father had her moved, and there was no location listed. I showed Kam and we both nodded. I handed her the iPad back, and we walked off.

"How did he even know that she was here?" I asked out loud, but to no one in particular.

"Good question," Kamery stated.

"That alone let me know that he was the one that caused all of this. No one knew that we were coming here but Allyn and Jazmine," I expressed. At that moment, all of the pieces of the puzzle were coming together.

"I just thought about something. Let's get to the house so that I can explain," I confessed as we headed to the car. The ride was quiet as we both were in our thoughts. When we pulled up at the house, we both jumped out. I was happy that everyone was in the same room with the exception of Kamery's mother and the kids. I was sure that

17

they were upstairs.

"When we went to the hospital, the records showed that Allynna's father moved her to an unlisted location which makes me think. How did he even know that she was here? The only people that knew we were there were Allyn, Jazmine, and —,"

"Justin," Kaye said, cutting me off.

"Correct. He has been acting funny since the day that you told him I got promoted. He is also originally from Cali. I remember that one day he was telling me his older brother was locked up in Cali and getting out soon. Ever since Terrell been dead that nigga been MIA. He was also Allyn's boy. Remember, Allyn was telling us that the nigga got too close to his daddy. As matter of fact, I'm about to call that nigga, and play his bluff," I stated. I pulled my phone out and dialed Allyn's phone number.

"What's good, Jeano," Allyn answered.

"Nothing… I was calling to see if you talked to Justin. I have been trying to get up with that nigga on some business, and he hasn't been answering."

"I haven't talked to that nigga since his brother got in town. He has been fucking with Angelo, though. I don't trust that nigga, and his brother looks sneaky as hell. I have just been laying low in New York since that shit happened to y'all. I know that he told Angelo that I've been fucking with y'all, so I know I'm next," Allyn explained. After he confided a couple of other things, I ended the call and directed my attention back to my family.

We all agreed that we would head back to Memphis, but Shan's mother had just gotten here, so we decided to stay for two more days so that she could see the city. There was no way that we would leave her here alone. I was so amped to get back so that I could end Justin's life. That was the first thing on my to-do list.

KAMERY

2 days later…

*M*y life was in shambles. It's like everyone was okay with how things were going but me. I never thought I would have had to bury my child. I was so ready to get to Memphis.

We had a couple of hours before it was time to go to the airport, so I figured that I would talk to my baby and see where her head was on all of the stuff that I had going on.

"Hey, beautiful."

"Hey, baby. What's up?" she said, bouncing KJ on her lap.

"Nothing… ready to get home so that I can marry you and make you a Mareno," I stated. She didn't immediately reply. She just blushed. I was so happy to see a smile on her face.

"I can't wait, baby. I'm so ready to start making another baby," she said, smiling.

"Baby, I love you so much. You always find the positive in everything that happens. What would I do without you? I'm so happy that God placed you in my life," I confessed. When I looked up, she had the biggest smile on her face, and KJ was laughing like he knew what was going on. Since the incident with the plane, we all decided to fly commercial.

"Go ahead and change him so that we can get going. We don't want to miss our flight. As a matter of fact, let's go see if Reagan and Kaye are ready. You know they always seem to be late for everything," I said, walking out the door. When I made it downstairs, all I could do was shake my head. Everyone was packed up and ready to go. I guess we weren't the only ones ready to roll.

"Where is Shay?" Shannon questioned as he was able to see my face.

"Changing KJ," I replied. I turned around and headed back to the room to grab our bags.

I knew they were all going to have something to say because we were the last ones to make it downstairs. When I got in the room, Shay and KJ were all ready to go, so I just grabbed the bags and headed down.

The ride to the airport was quiet. I guess everyone was lost in their thoughts. After boarding the flight, I felt uneasy. I guess it was because the last time we were on a plane, we were nearly killed. I just wished that my baby girl didn't have to pay the price for my mistakes. I knew that Shay blamed me, because I blamed me. If I would have handled my business, my daughter would still be alive.

I hadn't slept since. Every time I closed my eyes, all that I could see was my baby's lifeless body. What bothered me the most, was the fact that I couldn't get to her because I was trapped in the van. I wished I could give my life hers. She deserved to live her life. There were so many things that she would never get a chance to experience.

When KJ grew up, I would have to explain to him that I was the cause of his sister's death. I knew Shay wanted to have another baby, but I didn't think that I wanted to unless I got out of the game. After this, I was seriously considering passing this shit along to someone else. I had been thinking of a plan. I just needed to run it by my brothers and see what they thought.

Quitting the game almost made me feel like I was giving up, and that was just not something I could stomach. We had only been in charge for a little over a year. It seemed like we were being tested, because every time we solved one issue, another came up. I was just fed up with this shit. I was ending all of this shit when we got back, once and for all.

"Baby, can you hold KJ? I have to use the restroom," Shay said, pulling me from my thoughts. She handed me KJ and got up. When she got up, my damn eyes were trained on her big round ass. My baby was thick as fuck. A nigga would catch a case over her fine ass. Looking at her, you wouldn't know that she just had twins five months ago.

"What the hell are you thinking about? You're over here smiling and shit," Shay said as she sat back down next to me.

"Nothing... just thinking about how I'm going to get all in that ass when we get back home," I said while licking my lips.

"You're always thinking of something nasty," she giggled. Her smile was so intoxicating, and those eyes... they drove me crazy.

I didn't worry about giving her KJ back, because he was sleeping. I just laid him across my lap. She slipped right under me and fell asleep.

That alone made me feel bad. I had to fix this shit as soon as we got home.

SHANNON

$\mathcal{S}$eeing my sister and Kam made me want to be the man that Nyla and SJ needed. After seeing them lose a child, I didn't think I would have been that strong. Shay was such an amazing woman. She reminded me so much of my mother. No matter how bad things got, she always held her head up and stayed strong. She held Kam down as well as this whole family. I knew one thing. When we got back to Memphis, whoever did this would have hell to pay.

I had a fucked up feeling that there was more to this story than we thought. I knew that we would have haters, but damn. I didn't think that it would be this bad. There were so many people involved, but the first motherfucker to go needed to be Angelo. I had never seen a man like him. Who would want someone's whole family to suffer from some shit that he brought on himself? We needed to handle him ASAP.

"What are you thinking about, baby," Nyla asked me as she rubbed the side of my face. Her touch was so soft and gentle.

"Just handling things… shit that's going on so we can live the life that we should be living. You should be at the mall spending up all my money and walking around the house in one of the sexy ass PINK short outfits."

"You just want to be wearing that so you can feel all on me," She smiled.

"Yeah."

Just as she was about to say something to me, the flight attendant came by and smiled at me. I could tell by the look on Nyla's face that she was about to click. Before she could say anything, Reagan spoke up.

"Bitch, you must want your teeth knocked down your throat. Smile at my brother one more time like his wife is not sitting right next to him. You better hope you have a fucking job after I'm done. Now… go and do what they pay you to do," Reagan finished. The flight attendant looked like she was about to cry. The shit was funny as hell. One thing about my sisters and Nyla was that they had each other's backs, on matter what.

The rest of the plane ride was smooth. As soon as we landed, we all headed to Kamin's house since it was the most secure. I don't think I had ever been so happy to see Memphis in my life.

After we all got settled in, my mom and Kaye's mom cooked dinner. The shit was so good that all I wanted to do was go to sleep, but we all knew that wasn't going to happen. We had too much to do and not enough time. After dinner, all of the men headed down to the basement so that we could get the plan in line. On the way down, I couldn't help but to stare at Jeano. I knew he had to be going crazy, thinking about where Allynna could be. We still had people looking for her, but they kept coming up empty handed.

Once we got down in the basement, Kamery got straight to it.

"Allyn is our connection to Angelo. We all know that he was the

26

one to plant the bomb. No one else has the connections to do anything like that. With that being said, we need Allyn to be comfortable, but honestly, I don't trust him or Jazmine. I think they're hiding something. He was too calm when I talked to him on the phone. I'm going to have Shay and Reagan to ask her out to lunch. One thing about it, she wants to be in their good graces. There is no doubt about that. They know her weakness, so they will be able to get it out of her. Kaye, call Nuke and put it on speaker," Kam finished. Kaye did what he was told.

"What's good, Kaye Money?" Nuke answered.

"Nothing much… you alone, or do we need to call back?" Kamery asked,

"Nah, I'm at the crib. I just woke up," Nuke replied.

"When was the last time you saw Justin?" Kam asked.

"The other day. That nigga was riding in a Tesla, and I heard he moved his baby mama in a new spot," Nuke added. I couldn't believe this nigga was behind this shit the whole time. I remembered when that nigga's mama was sick, and we paid all of her medical bills with no question. After today, they were both going to wish that she died from cancer and not her son fuck ups.

"Call that nigga up. Act like you want to see what's up. Talk bad about us. I want to see what that nigga is going to say," Jeano said, taking a sip from his drink. I had to hold my laugh, because Jeano was a fool. He was going to say whatever he thought, and if you knew him, you will know that his facial expression showed exactly how he felt.

"Alright… hold on," Nuke said before clicking over to call Justin. I had no idea how this call would go, but I was ready to see what this fuck nigga had to say about us. I guess niggas just can't get trusted.

NUKE

*W*hen Kam told me that they were on the way back to Memphis, I knew some shit was about to pop off. One thing that I knew about Kam and Kaye was that were big on loyalty. You would think that niggas would know that, especially after what happened to Terrell.

In my eyes, this shit was to be expected since they offed Terrell. Justin was bound to get on some fuck shit. Justin and Terrell were like best friend. I know if a nigga offed my best friend, I would be out for blood. I kind of felt bad for my niggas, because they were some real niggas that look out for their team. I didn't know about these other niggas, but they make sure I ate good. They had been looking out for me since I was in high school. I trusted them with my life. One thing that I did know was that Justin should've known better than to cross these niggas.

"Nuke, do you hear me?" Kara, this chick that I be smashing every now and then said.

"Nah, I didn't. What did you say?" I asked, even though I really didn't care what she was saying. All I wanted was some head.

"I said I need some money to get my hair done," she yelled. This bitch clearly had me mixed up with one of these other niggas that she had been fucking. I didn't worry about replying. I just slipped my Timbs back on and walked out the door. As I got in the car, I put her on my block list. She had to be on some dope or some shit if she thought for a second that I would give her some money.

I had shit that I needed to handle for Kam, so it was time for me to dip. I made it the spot where Kam told me to meet him, and I saw Jeano's truck. I shook my head. That nigga was the quietest savage that I knew. I think the whole time that I had known him, I had seen him mad once, so when I heard him on the phone, pissed, that told me that shit was about to get ugly. I grabbed my blunt and headed in the warehouse.

"I see y'all don't do any playing. You found a new spot fast," I said as I lit the blunt that I had grabbed out the car.

"Never let them see you sweat, lil' nigga. You know we have to come back better that ever. When they hate, give them a reason to hate even more," Kaye said, taking my blunt out of my hand.

The more that I was around them, the more I looked up to them. Kam and Kaye always had each other's backs, and with Shan and Jeano behind them, they were a force to be reckoned with. They ran these Memphis streets.

"Can I ask y'all something?"

"Yeah, what's up?" Jeano answered.

"I've got this nigga that I've been cool with since I was a little nigga, but something doesn't seem right with him, and I just can't figure out what it is. He has been asking for me to put in a word for him with y'all so that he can get on, but I don't trust the nigga. There is no way that I will send him y'all way. The weird part is that he didn't start asking to get on until Justin's brother got out," I explained.

"So how is the nigga connected to Justin's brother?" Kam asked.

"I think his sister has a baby by the nigga or some shit like that."

"Find out what you can, and let us know," Jeano said.

"Okay."

"So look, Nuke… you've been rocking with us since you were a lil' nigga. Now is the time to show us how much you have learned. At some point, we have to pass the torch over. Jeano's girl is missing. We think that her dad kidnapped her. We also think that Justin is working with her dad. We need to find her. What would be the first thing that you do?" Kam asked.

I had to think this through, because I didn't want to give the wrong answer.

"First thing I need to know is where she was when she went missing."

"Columbia… she was in a coma, so there is no way that she could have walked out," Jeano said.

"Okay, well… we need to get the footage from the hospital. In order for her to get moved, someone had to be there to sign the paperwork. I haven't been seeing her brother around. I do know that the female that he was messing with is foul. I heard she was fucking his dad. I don't know how true that is, though. Have y'all asked him anything about his sister? If not, y'all should. He seemed shady to me. He had something to hide. If he didn't, there was no reason that he lived in ATL and came to

Memphis almost every day."

Just talking this through in my head was making me notice things that I have failed to see, like the fact that he and Justin hadn't been hanging lately. I remembered at one point, you couldn't see one without the other. Justin's brother seems to be the root of all of this.

"I remember… one day, we stopped at Justin's mama's house, and he was saying that his brother had been out for almost a year, and running shit in Miami. Why in the hell would he be telling everyone that his brother just got out the pen? That meant that they had been plotting this shit for a while. Does anyone know that y'all are back outside?" I asked.

"Nope… just the people that were on the trip," Kaye said, passing me the blunt.

"Okay, keep it that way. I'm going to get up with Justin. He said that he's at his mama's house. If you don't hear from me in an hour, come looking for me," I said before walking out the door. I knew just how to solve all of this.

ALLYNNA

3 weeks later (Sorrento, Italy)…

*I*t has been nearly a month since I left the hospital, and saying that I missed Jeano was an understatement. I missed the whole family. I knew that they will feel like I betrayed them, but this was the only way that I could save them.

When Angelo said that he would kill each and every one of them, I thought that he was lying until that plane blew up. They had been through enough I couldn't stand to see them suffer anymore. I wished that I could just reach out to them so that I could tell them how sorry I was. I hated being back here in Italy. It was like he brought me back here just so he can make my life a living hell. He had been keeping me locked in my room with no phone, and no computer… just me, my bed, and my thoughts. I have been reading day in and day out. I did have my kindle, but it didn't have an internet connection. I guess he cut the wireless off so that I couldn't connect. Now, I knew how men that went to prison felt. I couldn't even go out of the house.

I was just getting comfortable in my bed when I heard someone at the door. Shortly after that, the devil himself walked in the room.

"You still in here reading those dumb ass books?" Angelo asked, and he sat at the end of my bed. I didn't worry about replying. He was trying to piss me off.

"I thought you would like to know that your pussy ass brother contacted me, asking if I had seen you. I told him no... of course. I guess someone does care about your ungrateful ass," he sad with so much anger that his face was turning red. I just sat there in silence. There was no need to reply to him.

"So are you ready to tell me what you know?" he asked.

WHAP!!!!

He slapped me across the face. The shit was painful as hell, but I just sat there with no expression on my face. There was no way that I would let him know that he was hurting me. I guess he forgot about all of the training that he put me through, just in case someone did the exact thing that he is doing to me right now. When we were kids, he sent me and Allyn through SERE training because he wanted us to be prepared if someone every kidnapped us. He had done so much fucked up shit that he knew that it would happen one day. The other reason that I just sat there was because he hit like a bitch. After he hit me a few more times, I guess he realized that he wasn't hurting me, so he stopped and stomped out the room.

When he walked out, my thoughts drifted back to Jeano. I wondered if he was looking for me. I wished I could just let him know that I'm okay... just kiss him and tell him that I love him. I wondered if Reagan had given birth yet. If she had, I knew that he was so handsome. I just wished I could take it all back and start over. I would have told Jeano that Angelo had been contacting me, and what he had planned.

I wondered if they would ever forgive me.

I had been thinking of a way that I could get away, but I couldn't come up with anything. All I wanted was to be with my man. If I could just tell him where I was, I knew that he would come and get me. Maybe I could talk Angelo into letting me call Allyn. I know he would come for me. I hated this man with everything in me. I got disgusted every time that I looked at him. I just wished I could have saved my mom. Because of Angelo, I would never get to meet my real father. He was so selfish. I wondered if Angela knew that he killed our mother.

I started back reading until he walked in the room and just stood at the door. I knew just what to say to get his ass out my face.

"I hate you," I yelled. I guess he didn't expect me to say that, because he was just standing there with a weird look on his face.

"What did you just say, you little bitch?" he questioned as he dragged me by my hair. I was in so much pain, but I was not about to let him see that. I had to think fast. I needed a bargaining chip.

"If I tell you what I know, you have to let me get out of this house at least once a week. I will not run. I just can't take being in here all day like this," I pleaded.

"Okay, you give me information, and I will let you go out once a week, but my men will have to be with you," he agreed. He had to be the dumbest man alive to think that I wouldn't try and get away. Convincing his men to turn on him would be a no brainer. He treated them like crap already, so all I had to do was offer them money, and they would fold with ease.

"They know that it was you that blew upon the plane. They are planning to kill you. There is someone in your camp that's talking," I lied. I had no idea if they knew that he was behind all of this, but now that I knew he was, I wanted him dead even more. I could have died in that explosion. Just thinking of that day sent chills through my body. I still didn't know if everyone was okay. When I came out of the coma that I was in, I was in this exact room that I am in now. None of the nurses would talk to me. What if Jeano didn't make it?

"Okay, you can go next week and every other Wednesday," he finished. I didn't worry about replying. I just nodded and laid there on the floor. My head was killing me. All I wanted to do was lay down and go to sleep.

KAMERIN

I just knew that Shay and Reagan were going to be against us showing our faces. Surprisingly, they were all for it. We called up Nuke to let him know what was getting ready to go down.

"What's up, Kaye Money," he answered.

"Nothing much. Look… we're out here. The new product is in, so we're cleaning house. As of today, you need to be strapped at all times, because everyone has to go through you, Rue, and Rell. Get both of them, and meet us at the warehouse ASAP. I expect y'all there in twenty minutes. Don't disappoint me," was all I said before ending the call. We had let a lot of shit slide, and today, that would end. Today was the day that we showed them who was in control.

"Jeano, make the calls. All of the traps are closed for the day. We will be moving them all. See if your guy can get shit moved today. I've got the spots already. We need to shake some shit up. Have someone put the word out that we're not coming back I want to see if somebody tries to take over. That will show each and every disloyal person that is in our camp," I explained. He just nodded and pulled his phone out. Within fifteen minutes, he had everything in motion. That was what I loved about Jeano. He made shit happen fast.

Once we made it into the warehouse, Rell was pulling up, and Nuke's truck was already here.

"What's good, boss man?" Rell said as soon as we walked in. We all greeted each other as we walked to the door. After we walked in the door, he walked over and hugged Regan. He and Reagan were really close since he was her bodyguard. Right after that, Rue walked in with Kamina on his side. I couldn't do anything but laugh because she wouldn't let the man breath. Luckily for her, my mom and pops were cool with him being over all the time.

She ran over to me and hugged me like she didn't live in the house with me. Then, she ran over to Kam, Jeano, and Shan, doing the same. If you looked "spoiled brat" up on google, a picture of Kamina would pop up. I didn't see how Rue's ass dealt with her, but as long as he treated her right, he was good in my book.

"Got to get this money back in line," I replied to Rell. After we chopped it up for a minute, we got down to business.

"So we're splitting the city up between y'all three. No one talks to us. Everything goes through y'all. If there is a fuck up in your area, you are responsible. Count needs to be done every night, no matter what. Y'all have to have each other's backs. Look out for each other. Y'all will alternate weeks on doing inventory at the warehouse. No one... I mean no one is to know where this place is outside of the people in this room, my dad, and Uncle Ray. Is that understood?" I questioned, and everyone nodded their heads.

"If you can't trust someone on your team, then they have to roll, point blank. Remember... if they fuck up, it's on you. Can y'all handle that?" I asked. They all nodded.

"Now... you four," I said, referring to Shay, Reagan, Nyla, and Kamina.

"I found a spot downtown for y'all to open a clothing store. Rea... baby, I know that is something that you have always wanted to do, so here is your chance. We don't have many spots that sell designer clothes here, outside of Oak Hall, Superior, and that little spot in Oak Court. I thought y'all could call it Designz. I have a guy that can help y'all order in bulk.

Mina, you're going to work just like everybody else. You handle kids. Shay, you do Men, and Reagan, you do Women. Nyla, you know what to do. We will go and look at the building when we leave here. Lastly, let's get everyone set up for the alarm system," I said, walking toward my office.

After we all set our code up, we all loaded into our rides and headed out. I made sure that everyone had their own code so that it would capture who goes in and out of the warehouse. No two people had the same code, so that way, nobody would get mixed up. After we were done with that, we headed to the store. The ride there was quiet, outside of Kamina and Rue giggling the whole damn time.

When we made it to the building, Reagan and Shay's faces lit up. I knew they were happy, because this was something that they had been talking about for the past year.

"I swear... when I get me a woman, I'm going to spoil her just like y'all spoil them," Nuke said as she watched the women walk through the store in excitement.

"Y'all set the bar so high that I don't think I will ever find a good woman," Nuke spat.

"You will. Trust me, and when you do, make sure you keep her," Kamery told him as he walked off toward Shay. I walked up to Reagan and kissed her on the forehead. Just seeing my baby smile after all that we had been through in the past couple of months made it all worth it.

"Baby, we need to go and check on Brands. We haven't been there since we have been home. I've been talking to Brittany every day, but we need to show our faces," Reagan said. We all walked toward the door. I nodded in agreement, because when hadn't been to Brands, so that need to be a done.

"I'm going to ride with y'all and leave my car here," Nuke said. That was one thing that I liked about him. He was ready to learn and soak up knowledge. We all loaded the sprinter and headed to Brands.

The whole ride there, we tripped and cracked jokes. Nuke was a real stand-up guy. For him to be as young as he was, he had his head on straight. He was in the streets, but he was also in college, and the kid was smart as hell. I can see us passing this down to him one day.

NUKE

I know it sounded kind of kiddy as hell, but I wanted to be just like these folks when I got their age. They were a group of power couples. They were making money moves together. That was what I wanted, in all honesty. I was tired of fucking all these different women. I just wanted one woman. Most would say that I am too young to be trying to settle down, but I'd say fuck whoever thinks that. Seeing all of them so happy and in love made me feel uneasy, but all in all, I was happy for all of them… especially my best friend, Rue. Rue and Rell had been through so much, and they both deserved someone that would make them happy.

When we pulled up to Brands, there was a line around the building which was to be expected since it was a Saturday morning. One thing about Memphis niggas was that they would be in line for the new Js. Half of these niggas living at home with their mama, but they were worried about getting the new Js.

We all got out of the van and headed to the store. As soon as I walked in and looked at the girl behind the counter, I couldn't move. I was stuck standing in the doorway. I don't think I had ever seen someone so beautiful in my life. Her smile was so mesmerizing. She had her full lips painted red, and that shit alone had me ready. That dress she was wearing was fitting lovely, but tight enough for me to see how fat and round her ass was.

"Damn, nigga! Pick your lip up," Shannon said, pulling me from my thoughts as he pushed past me.

"Aye, Shan. What's her name?" I asked.

"I don't know. Shit, I only come here when I need to. That's Kamina's best friend, so go and ask one of them," he said, walking toward the back of the store. I just stood there for another few minutes before the girl at the counter looked up, and we made eye contact. She blushed, then quickly looked off, and I headed to the back so that I could find Mina or somebody that could tell me more about her.

I caught Nyla right in time, because she was about to start helping a customer.

"Ny, what's her name?" I asked. At first, she didn't answer. She just rolled her eyes and handed the man a pair of shoes to try on.

"Brittany… She is a good girl, Nuke, so if you're looking for a smash, just keep pushing," she fussed. That alone made me want her more, because if Nyla was vouching for her, then that meant she was worth the hassle. I didn't reply. I just headed to the back where the rest of the men were. They were discussing some shit about the traps, but all I could focus on was Brittany. I was watching her on the camera that was outside Kamerin's office.

"Damn… why don't you just go out there and talk to her instead of watching her from the camera like a stalker," Jeano said, laughing.

"Nigga, I ain't going out there so that she can embarrass me. Besides, if I go out there fucking with her, Shay is going to curse my ass out. I can't take that chance," I said, still staring at the camera screen. I planned on talking to her. I was just waiting on the perfect time.

"The stack of shoes behind her is getting lower and lower, so I know at some point she will have to go to the back to get some more. I will make my move then," I said. They all just busted out laughing.

"You're really plotting on how you're going to talk to her. Who does that, nigga? One of those niggas out there are going to snatch her up, while you're back her plotting and shit," Kam laughed. He knew what he was doing to her. He knew there was no way that I would let that happen.

"Damn, I didn't think about that. That's going to be my wife," I said, getting up and walking toward the front of the store.

"This nigga has lost it. Wait until I tell bae this," Rue yelled as I was walking out of Kaye's office. On the way up, I passed Nyla in the stock room.

"Remember what I told you, Nuke," she said as she pulled shoes out and sat them on a cart. As I walked to the counter, the dude that checked out was asking her for her number.

"Nah, lil' homie. She's good," I said while walking up. She didn't say anything. She just smiled and handed him his bag.

"Have a great day. Your receipt is in the bag," was all she said before handing him the bag. There was no damn way that I was about give a nigga the chance to get with my girl. Well, she's not my girl yet, but she will be soon. She rang the customer up and bagged the shoes. Every time I looked up, I could see her and Mina talking with their eyes.

"Nuke, what the hell are you doing up here?" Shay asked as she opened the register next to Brittany.

"Making sure none of these niggas try and get over on my new boo," I replied. Shay just laughed.

"How are you just going to make me your boo. How do you know I don't have a man?" Brittany asked, catching me off guard. I didn't worry about replying, because if she did have a nigga, that shit was about to end. After the line died down a little, Shay took over and told her to go on break. As soon as we made it in the break room, she sat down.

"Thanks for having my back. I get so tired of guys doing that," she said as I handed her a bottle of water.

"No thanks needed. I don't need a nigga all over my woman," I said, sipping from my water.

"Your woman?" she said as if she was surprised.

"Yeah... my woman."

"When did I become all of that? I don't even know your name, and you're calling me your woman. How does that work?" she questioned.

"Sorry, baby girl. I'm Brian, but everyone calls me Nuke," I said as I extended my hand. She shook my hand and smiled.

"Well, Nukie... I'm Brittany, but everyone calls me Brittany," she said while laughing. I couldn't do anything but laugh. There was nothing like a woman that could make you laugh.

"So what we eating for dinner tonight, my new woman," I laughed.

"Since I have a new man that I didn't know about, I figured that he can take me to Houston's for dinner," she said, sipping from her water. Apparently, she didn't know who she was fucking with. I guess she thought saying that would run me away, but I was going to have to show her.

"Cool with me. Just save your number in my phone, and I will call you when I'm on my way," I said, handing her my phone. She locked her number in, and went back to the front. I headed back to Kaye's office.

After we were done at Brands, they dropped me back at my car. I headed home so that I could be on time picking Brittany up from work. I made it home just in time to catch the cleaning lady so that I could have her to clean my guest room. My brother was coming in town for a few days.

My older brother, Kyle, was the total opposite of me. We both were educated, but he is one of those Wall Street, goody to shoe niggas. Don't get shit twisted. That nigga could get down with the best.

I was heading to the bathroom to get in the shower when my phone rang. I looked down to see who it was, but ended up dropping my damn phone.

"Yo," I answered.

"Hey, Nuke," a familiar voice said from the other end of the phone. I knew the voice. I just couldn't think of who it was.

"Who is this?" I questioned.

"Damn, you forgot about me that quickly?" the female voice said. I still couldn't put my finger on the voice, and that shit was making me mad.

"When you are ready to tell me who you are, then call me back," I said before hanging up. Whoever it was, called back, but I didn't worry about answering. I just headed to the shower. When I got out of the shower, I got dressed and headed to pick Brittany up from work. I pulled up a few minutes early, so I decided that I would check my messages sine I had six unread. They all had to be from who called me, because I had cleared my messages before getting in the shower.

(901)550-3555: Nuke, why you hang up on me?

(901)550-3555: Nuke, this is Cara. Can you answer the phone?

(901)550-3555: I just need to tell you that I'm pregnant

(901)550-3555: I know it's out of the blue, but I just want my child's father to be in his life

(901)550-3555: Can you call me so that we can talk?

The last one was a picture of an ultrasound. I just deleted all of the messages and blocked the number. Apparently, she didn't know that I already knew she was pregnant by this nigga from the hood named Chris. She must have thought I was a fool. I laughed out loud, because this bitch really was trying me.

BRITTANY

$\mathscr{I}$ had been nervous all day, waiting on Nuke to come back and get me. It was something about him that made me nervous. I had been around a million different men, but there was something about him. He made me smile on the inside. I had been watching the clock on the door for the past hour. Shay and Mina had been teasing me since he walked out of the car earlier.

"Girl, if you don't stop looking at the damn door and count that drawer. That boy is going to come," Shay fussed. I couldn't help but laugh, because I knew that he would come. Just thinking about him was driving me crazy. It was like his cologne was lingering in my nose. I don't know what kind of cologne it was, but whatever it was, I wanted him to wear it every time he was around. As if on cue, he was pulling up as soon as we were locking the door. Normally, Kamina would take me home.

He was looking so good. I slowly walked to the car and looked at my phone. I didn't want him to see me blushing as he got out to open the door for me. I hadn't ever had a man to open doors for me. Hell, I don't think I'd ever seen my dad open a door for my mother.

"Hey, beautiful," he smiled, pulling me in for a hug. I hugged him back and got in the car. He was winning me over big time. He even made sure my seat belt was buckled before closing the door after I got in. Again, that scent was invading my nose.

"How was your day, baby girl?" he asked me, catching me off guard.

"Ummm… it was okay, I guess."

"Tell me about you, ma," he said, catching me off guard again. I never had someone want to know about me. Honestly, this was my first date. I had never been out with a guy. I'm sure if my dad knew that I was out with him, he would've killed me.

"Well… I'm eighteen. I live with my parents. I go to Central High School. I'm an only child. I have been working at Brands since I was sixteen. I don't have many friends, because my dad didn't allow me to have any growing up," I confessed.

"So what do you like to do? What is your passion? You going to college?" he asked. He was asking questions that I hadn't even thought about. I just sat there for a minute and thought about what he asked.

"Well, I don't know about college. My parents don't really have the money to send me. I have always wanted to go, but the money that I have saved up, I will have to use to get a place to stay after graduation. I love kids. I want to be a math teacher or accountant, because I love math as well. I don't know what my passion is at this moment. I haven't really thought about it. What about you?" I asked.

"Let's see… my passion is whatever I'm focused on at the moment, and right now, it's you. I like learning new things and math. I'm currently in college. My major is accounting with a minor in business, so I guess that is something that we have in common," he finished. I just blushed. The rest of the ride was quiet, and we held hands. Every few minutes, I would see him glance over at me and smile.

Before I knew it, we pulled up at Houston's. When we walked in, he told the lady we had reservations. She walked us to a room in the back of the restaurant. The room was closed off from the restaurant. When we walked in, I was taken away. It was perfect.

"How did you know that Sunflowers are my favorite?" I asked as I tried to smell each and every one of them.

"Let's just say that I did my research," he confessed while smiling. He was too cute for me.

"I see you pulled out all the stops," I said as he pushed my seat to the table. He was such a gentleman.

"Nah, ma. This is something small. There is bigger to come. Just rock with a nigga. You will see," he giggled. He was doing all the things my dad told me that no man would every do. Let me give a little insight on my life so that you will understand my struggles and what I'm going through.

I'm the only child from my dad. I have an older sister on my mother's side, but I have never met her. I have asked my mom about her, but she never tells me anything, so in my eyes, it's just me. My life has been sheltered from the day that I was born. I didn't go to school until I was in the eighth grade. That when I met Kamina.

I ain't allowed to participate in sports or anything that happens outside of school hours. My dad said that he didn't want the outside world to influence me and make me a hoe like my mama. That was something that I never understood, because my mother never left the house unless we all went as a family, so when did she have time to be a hoe?

The only thing that I have experienced is my dad beating my mom's ass. That was a daily thing. I never really understood why he did it, but not a day passed that he didn't beat her. That why I have been saving up to move when I'm done with school. I hated to leave my mommy there with the monster, but I had to look out for me.

Growing up, I always wanted to go to college. All of that changed the day that I got my ass beat for saying that I was going to graduate from college and open an accounting firm. If I'm thinking right, it was my tenth grade year, so long story short, my life was a kind of fucked up.

The rest of dinner was amazing. We were talking about everything that came to mind. We were so into each other that I didn't notice that it was almost eleven. I knew my dad was going to beat my ass when I got home. Just thinking about it made me dread having dinner with him. Apparently, he could feel the change in my mood that I was trying my best to hide. I just knew that I wanted to be able to go to school for a few days after my dad beat my ass. He always made me stay home so that the school wouldn't know that he was beating the hell out of me.

"What's wrong, baby girl?" Nuke asked, grabbing my hands. That's another thing about me. When I got nervous, my hands would sweat.

"Nothing… why do you say that," I asked.

"Your whole attitude has changed, and your hands are sweating," he stated.

"Tell me what's wrong, and don't lie to me," he said in a firm tone. It was like one of the ones my dad used, but there was compassion in Nuke's voice.

"Nothing... it's just that my dad will be upset that I have been out so late," I confessed.

"Does he beat you, Brittany?" Nuke asked, catching off guard once again. I did not expect him to ask me that. It really put me in a bad space, because he just got done telling me that he hated to be lied to. On the other hand, Kamina already told me how ruthless he was. If I told him the truth, he would probably kill my dad and kill my mother for letting it happen. I didn't reply. I just dropped my head. I guess that told him all that he needed to know.

"Don't ever do that, Brittany. I don't know what you're used to, but I'm going to show you how a queen is to be treated. Look people in the eyes. When you don't do that, people lose respect for you. Now, I'm going to drop you off at home and walk you in the door. Call me if he touches a hair on your head. If I don't get a call within ten minutes after I drop you off, I'm coming back, and I'm sure you know how I get down. Now... let's roll," he said, throwing three hundred dollar bills on the table. We walked to the car, hand in hand. I felt like I was on top of the world. If I didn't like him before, I definitely did now.

The ride to my house was quiet. I was afraid. No matter what he said, I knew what was about to happen, especially since it was going on midnight.

When he pulled into the driveway, I grabbed the door so that I

51

could get out the car.

"You never open a door for yourself when I'm around. Do you understand me, Brit Brat?"

I just sat back and waited for him to come around and open the door for me. My hands were sweating like crazy, especially because my dad was standing at the door just watching us. He opened the door and helped me out, grabbing my backpack from my hands. Nuke walked me to the door and waited for me to go in. I could tell by the look on my dad's face that he was about to say something stupid.

Before I could get in the door good, my dad was snatching me by the collar of my shirt.

"Bitch who the fuck do you think you are, coming to my house at midnight. I know you have been seeing me calling you. You're out here being a hoe like your mama. You think that nigga wants you? He doesn't give a fuck about you!" my father yelled. Before I knew it, the front door was flying open, and Nuke was walking in. He rushed over my dad and grabbed him by the collar of his sweater.

"Nigga, if you ever put your hands on her again, I will kill you. I don't know what type of man treats his wife and daughter this way, but make it the last day. If I find out that you even breathe on either of them too hard, I will fucking blow your brains out," Nuke yelled with his gun to my dad's head. I wasn't the least bit scared. At that moment, I knew that I loved Nuke. No one had ever stood up for us, not even my uncles. They all knew that my dad beat the hell out of us and hadn't done anything about it.

My dad looked like he was about to shit a brick. I wanted to laugh so badly. Apparently, me and Nuke could feel each other's vibe because he looked directly at me and smiled. After he was done talking, he dropped my dad and he fell to the floor. I just looked at them both and walked over to Nuke.

"Baby, can I spend the night with you? I don't feel safe here," I stated.

"No question," he said, before walking back to the door. "I will be waiting in the car, baby."

I just walked up the stairs and grabbed some clothes for school before I headed to the car. Who would have known that this would be the start of my week?

JEANO

A week later...

$\mathcal{I}$ was doing my best to get adjusted to life without Allynna, but the shit was hard. A nigga was hungry as shit. I felt like I hadn't eaten in forever, even though I had eaten every damn day. I just hoped that she was okay. All I wanted to do was get my baby back home with me. I knew that she was not dead. I could feel in my heart that she was okay. I just needed to hear it from her. I had tapped out all of my sources which meant I would never find where he was hiding her.

I was laying back on the bed, and my eye went to her Kindle. Reading was one of her favorite things to do. I got out the bed and powered it on. When it was fully powered on, I scrolled through the books that she had downloaded. One caught my eye, and that alone let me know that she was okay. She had been talking about the book titled *Blazing for His Love* by some chick named Vaneecia. That book had been added to her cloud on Kindle. I felt so relieved knowing that she was alive. Now, all I needed to do was think of a way that I could get her back home to me. Just as I was about to go shower so that I could go and show Reagan what I found, my phone rang, and a picture of my nephew, Kamden, popped up on my screen.

"I was just about to get dressed and come through," I said, answering the phone.

"How long will that be?" she asked.

"Like thirty minutes… Aye, do those things that y'all be reading the books on have an internet connection?" I asked.

"You talking about the Kindle?"

"Yes, whatever the fuck they're called," I replied.

"Why do you ask that? You about to start reading?" she asked, trying to be funny. She knew I hated reading. Hell, I hated when they read. Somebody could be out to kill them, and they wouldn't know shit if they were reading. That shit took all of their focus.

"Hell nah. I got one more question, though."

"I'm listening," she replied.

"Remember when we were on the plane… you and Llynna were talking about that book that y'all were waiting on to release."

"Yeah… the name of it is *Blazing for His Love*. What about it?" she asked.

"What day did it release?" I questioned. I was hoping it was in the past few days or so, that way I could have the IP that the book was downloaded from traced. I knew that she was logged in with her account so that should be an easy trace for Wizz.

"Last week. Why?" she questioned. I knew that was coming.

"Her Kindle is here. I remember she left it here before we went to Columbia. Remember… y'all were making fun of her because I

56

wouldn't buy her one in the airport. That book that I was just asking about is on her cloud, and if that's the case, then she is alive. I can see if maybe Wizz can find out the IP were the book was downloaded, and I can find my baby and bring her back home. It also can lead us to Angelo, since we all know that he is probably that one that has her," I explained.

"Okay, well hurry up and get her. I will update everyone else on your findings, inspector gadget," she said while laughing. We ended the call, and I headed straight to the shower. I was amped that I was about to find my baby. After I showered, I threw on a tan Polo sweat suit, and my white and tan Uptempos, grabbed my white Yankees fitted and headed out the door.

When I made it to Kamin's house where everyone was staying, I jumped out my truck with Allynna's Kindle in hand. I was so happy when I saw Wizz's ugly ass lime green Lambo in the driveway. I didn't know what made this low-key ass nigga get a lime green car. You could spot that motherfucker from a mile away. I guess it was a good thing that he was low-key. I just hoped that nigga didn't ever get in any trouble. If he did, he'd be fucked.

When I walked in the door, a smile crept across my face as I watched my family. We had been through so much, and to see us all still standing tall made me happy. Before I could get in the door good, Shayla was taking the Kindle from my hands.

"Let's see what the last book that she read is, or if she is in the middle of reading one now," Shay said, scrolling through the Kindle.

"Bingo! She is reading *Can't Hide from Love* by Bianca."

"How do you know what she is reading?" I asked.

"See… this little thing here is telling you the point that you last left off, and if you open the book, then it will take you to the last page opened. I know a way that we can let her know that we have her Kindle. Hand me your laptop, Wizz," she demanded.

"Never mind. Just create a document telling her that we are looking for her. I can upload the document to her Kindle. She will be able to see it. Here is the email address that you have to send it to," she explained.

She showed him something on the screen, and then had him to hack into her Kindle account so that they could upload the document. A few minutes later, the document was showing on her Kindle. That shit was amazing. I would have never thought that this little ass thing would be able to do that, but I was down for whatever it took to get her back here to me.

Shay had uploaded a document onto the Kindle. It was crazy all of the things that you could do with technology.

After we were done with that, I headed to the hood just to show my face and see what the word on the streets was. I knew niggas had been talking. I just wanted to know what they had been talking about. I pulled up and saw Kev. Kev was one of my men that nobody other than family knew was on my team. That's just how I wanted it to be, that way niggas would talk around him.

"What's good, nigga? I heard you were in town. I just hadn't seen you," he lied in front of the group of niggas that he was chopping it up with. All of the niggas shook up with me and finished their conversation.

"Aye, Kev. Who has that good shit," I said, letting him know that I needed to talk to him.

"My nigga, Harry. I can take you over there to get some, if you want me to," he said, excusing himself from the conversation. Once we were in my truck, that nigga started spilling the beans.

Apparently, the nigga from Miami was indeed Justin's brother, and Justin is Jaxon Shayla ex-boyfriend cousin. They had a deal with Jaxon, and since he couldn't uphold his end, they were forcing Jaxon's daddy to uphold it. That is where the problems came in. His dad was out of the game, and the only way that he could get anything in was through us. I couldn't wait to get to Kamin's house so that I could feel them in, especially Kamin.

REAGAN

$\mathcal{I}$ really hoped Jeano found Allynna. I know it may sound crazy, but I missed her. We had grown really close in the past couple of months, and it was really getting to me that they couldn't find her. Outside of her being gone, I couldn't be any happier. I had my husband, my son, and the rest of my family. I still hadn't gotten over the shock of Jeano being my brother, and hearing him talk about my grandmother made the think of her. That was something that I hadn't done in years. I wanted to call her, but I was more than sure that she wouldn't accept my calls. The last time that she tried to reach out to me, I blew her off. I wished I would have though, because even though my mother never loved me, I knew that my grandmother did. I just couldn't get over the fact that she knew what was going on and didn't try to stop it.

I had been in our room, organizing Kamden's clothes when Kamina came in the room looking crazy. I knew something was wrong, because she was fiddling with her fingers. I'd learned that was something that she did when she was nervous.

"What's wrong, Mina?" I questioned as I pulled myself up off the floor so that I could take a seat next to her on the chase. Mina was such a sweet girl, and I knew she was about to burst with all of the shit that was going on.

"I'm listening, Kamina," I spoke in a firm tone.

"I think I'm ready," she mumbled. I know she wasn't saying what I thought she was. Kamina had lost her damn mind. I was going to kill Rue's ass. He had my baby's head all fucked up. As bad as I wanted to curse her ass out, I was happy that she trusted me enough to come and tell me.

"What makes you so sure that you are ready?" I asked. She didn't say anything. She just looked down at her hand.

"Hello? What makes you so sure that you ready to pop that pussy for a real nigga," I laughed. I was laughing so hard that I didn't realize Shay had walked in the room.

"What the hell are you laughing at, and who is popping their pussy for a real nigga?" Shay questioned as she climbed in the bed. I wanted to tell her what Kamina had just confessed, but it wasn't my place.

"Umm... I was just telling Rea that I think I'm ready," Kamina said.

"Ready for?" Shay questioned. That shit was funny because Kamina was Shay's pride and joy. In Shayla's eyes, that girl could do no wrong.

"To have sex! Damn, Shay! Stop acting dumb. The girl is almost grown," I fussed. Kamina would be eighteen and graduate from high school in a few months. They all acted like the damn girl was fifteen. She wasn't ever going to grow up in their eyes.

"And what makes you think that you are ready, baby girl?" Shay asked in a calm but serious tone. I could tell by the look in her eyes that this shit was killing her.

"I just do. I love him, and he is the one that I want to share that moment with," Kamina pleaded.

"Have y'all talked about it?" I asked.

"No, he has never talked to me about sex at all. He doesn't even bring it up," Mina replied. She had a sparkle in her eyes when she said that. At that point, I was more than sure that she would stand firm on her decision to get with Rue.

"When do you plan on doing this?" I asked.

"I was thinking Prom night."

I felt a sign of relief, because prom was not for another month and a half. That would give her time to really think it out before she did it. I just didn't want her to have sex with him, and then he hurt her. I would have to kill him, and I didn't want to have to do that.

"Mina, I just want you to be sure that is what you want to do. Don't do anything that you don't want to do. Just be sure that it's what *you* want to do," Shay said, walking in the bathroom. Mina was just sitting there like she was thinking about what Shay had just said. I just hoped that she was making the right decision.

Just as I was about to get up, my phone started ringing. I looked down to see Kamerin calling, and a smile crept on my face.

"Hey, baby," I answered.

"Hey, baby. I just wanted to check on my lil' man and see what my beautiful wife was doing," he replied. It was like each day I gained more and more love for him. I would have never thought that I would be married with a child at this point in my life. I guess that goes to show that you never knew what God had in store for you.

"I will be there as soon as I find a house that I want you to look at. I know pops thinks us being there is safe, but I miss having my own space. I have to be all quiet when we be fucking and shit. That's not working for me. I like to hear you scream my name, and walk around naked. That's what I'm used to, and that's what I want. Being almost thirty and living with my parents is not a good look," he fussed.

I don't think I'd heard him fuss like that in a while, so I knew that he was serious. I just listened. I didn't reply, because if I would have, then we would be arguing, and I didn't have time for that today. It was like if I disagreed with him, then it was World War III. After he was done fussing, I ended the call and reverted my attention back to Kamina.

"You must be texting Rue, because you're over here smiling hard as hell," I said, trying to look at her phone so that I could see if she was texting him. She locked her screen when she saw me look.

"Damn, Rea! You nosey. Don't worry about me and my phone. Worry about why my brother was cursing your ass out just a minute ago," she said, laughing. I didn't even worry about replying to her. I just got up and walked out the room. I caught an attitude real quick.

SHAYLA

I was happy to be back in Memphis, but living at Kamin's house was about to run me the fuck crazy. Now don't get me wrong… his house was the bomb, but I wanted to be at my own house. I wanted my own space. I was still in our room, waiting for Kam to get here so that I could tell him how I was feeling, but as always, he was taking forever to make it back. I needed to change KJ, so I got up to do that. As soon as I was done, Kam walked in.

"Hey, baby. What are you and my lil' man doing?" he asked, taking KJ from my hands.

"I was changing his lil' shitty ass. He shits more than anybody I know," I fussed.

"Fall off my baby, Shay," Kamery laughed walking out the room. Now that he had KJ for a minute, all I wanted to do was soak in the tub. I ran myself some bath water. When it was done, Kam walked back in the room. I just rolled my eyes. He was forever passing KJ off to his mom. I knew she should be tired of kids. Every time you looked around, the kids were in her and Kamin's room.

"Can I get in with you?" he asked, taking his shirt off. I didn't reply. I just focused back on my Kindle. I guess he didn't get the hint, because I looked up, and this nigga was naked as the day he came out the womb. I just shook my head.

"What the hell you talking your clothes off for? I didn't tell you that you could get in the tub with me," I said while laughing. He didn't reply. He just walked toward me and kissed me softly on the lips. As always, my lady box started flowing which is crazy because I was in the water. He picked me up out the tub and sat down, then sat me on his lap.

"Baby, I'm ready for you to be my wife. When are you going to start planning the wedding?" he asked as he kissed my neck.

"When we're in our own house and not your parent's house," I said with an attitude. I really didn't mean to have an attitude, but that was just how it came out. I was tired of this shit.

"Where is that attitude coming from Shayla?" he questioned.

"I'm sorry, baby. I don't mean to have an attitude. I'm just ready to be in my own house. Baby, can we please go look for a house today. Please, baby?" I begged.

"Soon as we move, I will hire a wedding planner so that we can get things started," I finished. He was smiling like he had won the lottery.

"Okay, baby," I blushed.

"I wanted to talk to you about Jazmine. I think she is lost in all this shit going on. Something is telling me that Allyn is using her. I don't trust Allyn," he explained.

"I will call her so that I can meet with her. I will know if she is lying once I can get her alone with Reagan," I confessed. One thing for sure was that we had been friends a long time, and I knew her. I knew that she never looked you in the eyes, and played with her hair when she was nervous about something.

"Thanks, baby."

We sat in the tub together until the water got cold. We talked about everything under the moon. We even decided that our wedding theme would be black tie. Life was finally coming together.

When we were done bathing, we headed downstairs where everyone else was. I was so happy to see Jeano, because I hadn't seen him since he brought Allynna's Kindle over.

"Hey, Jeano. You okay?" I asked, hugging him.

"Nah, sis. I'm not okay. I'm worried about my baby. I have used every source I have, and I still haven't found her. I can't even find Angelo's address. It's like he disappeared. I'm not crazy. I know he exists, but it looks as if he doesn't. I bought myself a plane ticket. I'm going to Italy to find her if it's the last thing that I do," Jeano explained.

I wanted to laugh so badly, but I knew that he was dead serious. I couldn't be mad, because if the shoe was on the other foot, I would be looking for Kam as well. I just hoped that he found her. I missed her silly ass.

We all talked for a while after he left. Kam and I headed back to our room to start looking at houses on his iPad. After jotting down a few that we liked, I headed to get KJ so that I could put him down to bed.

"Hey, mommy's baby," I said, walking in the den.

"Hey, dad. I didn't know that you were here," I added after seeing my dad sitting at the bar.

"I just got here, baby doll," my dad said, walking over to give me a hug.

"I was coming to get KJ so that I could put him down for bed, but I know that's not happening now. Just call my phone when y'all want me to come back and get him," I said before heading back to my room. I would have never known that Kamin was the best friend that my dad talked about when we were growing up. I guess Memphis was smaller than I thought. I guess God saw fit for us all to be one big family.

Once I was in the room, I grabbed my phone to scroll Instagram. It was the same shit that I always saw. I was just about to close the app until I saw a picture of Kam and Kaye with the caption MCM's. I instantly got mad.

"Too bad it's only a crush… what's your face going to be if you post my man again," I commented. I just laughed and went Reagan's room.

"Look at this bullshit," I said, handing Rea my phone. She looked at it and handed me my phone. She picked her phone up.

"Girl, I don't have time. You are crazy as hell. I bet that hoe over there is mad as hell," she laughed. I don't know who these hoes thought they were playing with, but they had better find somebody else's nigga to play with. Those hoes could get the business about bae. I closed Instagram and proceeded to text Jazmine.

JAZMINE

"*B*aby, dinner is ready," I yelled up the stairs to Allyn.

"Alright, baby. I'm headed down now," he yelled back. Since he was on the way down, I decided to go ahead and fix his plate. I was just happy that he didn't wake up with an attitude. Lately, he had been so unhappy. I knew it was because of all the stuff going on with his father, but that was no reason for him to mistreat me. I had been doing my best to stay out of his way. He wasn't having it, though. Every time I found something to keep myself busy and out his way, he found a reason to call my damn name.

"Hey, beautiful," Allyn said as he walked in the kitchen.

"Hey, baby," I said, kissing him as I put the plates on the table.

"Allyn, I haven't said grace, baby," I said to him as he attempted to start eating.

"I'm sorry, baby. It just looks so good," he said while smiling. Allyn was such a charmer. After we said grace, we ate dinner. Afterward, he went to his office, and I cleaned up the kitchen. One thing I could say that I loved about Allyn was that he was clean just like me. Our house was so clean that you could eat off the floor.

After twenty minutes of cleaning, I was headed to my office so that I could finish some graphics I was working on. I had been working on small projects so that I could get my business off the ground. I'd been into graphics since I was a kid. I just never had the time to work on them. Now that I was in a good stable place, that was all I was focused on. I had done a logo for Allyn and one of his friends saw it. I had been booming since. There was so much business here in Atlanta, and I loved it. It kept me busy, and out of his way.

I was getting adjusted in my chair when my text notification went off.

Shayla: *What's up, chick??*

Me: *Girl, nothing... working on some graphics*

Shayla: *That's what's up. I might need you to do some shit for me*

Me: *Yeah, I can do that. We should meet for lunch Friday*

Shayla: *Cool, meet me at the old spot*

Me: *Girl, I haven't have been to Westy's in years. Cool with me. Is Rea coming?*

Shayla: *Yep*

Me: *Ok... see you tomorrow*

I was so happy she agreed to meet. I just knew she was going to say no when I asked her to meet. I missed them so much. I didn't have many friends and really didn't want any. I'd rather just repair my relationship with them.

"What are you smiling about, love?" Allyn asked, walking into my office.

"Nothing... Shay agreed to meet with me. I just want my friends

70

back. Baby, I miss them so much. I just hope that she can forgive me. I did so much wrong to her, even though I really didn't try to. They are all that I have, especially since my parents hate each other so much that they forgot they have a child.

I remember the first time my dad hit my mom. I ran to Shay's house with nothing but my PJ's… no shoes, and no coat. It was freezing outside I know it had to be at least thirty degrees outside. I was so scared to go home, but her dad took me home and talked to my dad. I don't know what he said, but my dad never hit my mom again. I don't think I ever got a whooping after that. I bet her dad was so disappointed in me," I cried. I hadn't thought about that part of my life in so long. I had pushed it as far in the back of my mind as I could.

"Baby, all you can do is be yourself. Either she will forgive you, or she won't. I'm here for you," he consoled me. The way he was rubbing my thigh was turning me on in a major way. His had eased over to the panties and rubbed my kitty through my panties. That shit was driving me crazy. I let out a soft moan, and that was all he needed to hear. He pulled my panties to the side and slowly rubbed his finger against my clit.

"Mmmmm… baby, you know I love when you do that," I moaned. A smile crept on his face as he started moving his finger faster across my clit. This man had a way of driving me crazy, especially when it came to sex. I could feel myself getting ready to climax, and apparently he did too, because he slipped one finger in me as he fingered my clit. Just as I was about to climax, he dropped down to his knees and attacked my kitty with his tongue.

"Baby, what are you doing to me?" I moaned as he sucked on my clit. I was doing my best to hold back the orgasm that was about to erupt.

"Why are you holding that nut back baby?" he asked, looking into my eyes. He had the most beautiful gray eyes ever. Every time I looked directly into his eyes, they put me in a daze.

He started fingering me and licking my clit at a fast pace, making me squirt all over his face. It was like that shit took all the energy out of me. I was done for the night. At least I thought I was. He picked me up, and sat me on his lap.

"Shit! Allyn… baby! What are you trying to do?" I mumbled as he entered me.

"Trying to put a baby in you," he smirked. As bad I wanted to reply to him, I couldn't. He was hitting my spot with force, and that shit was killing me. I never knew pain could feel so good.

"Baby … I'm … about to…. Mmmm, cum!" I moan so loud that I'm sure the housekeeper and neighbors could hear me. I really hated having sex when the housekeeper was here, because I didn't want her to be looking at me crazy, but Allyn didn't care who was here. He wanted it when he wanted it.

"Shit, Jazz. Baby, I'm about to cum too. Fuck!" he moaned as he released his kids inside of me. I was no good after that. All I want to do at this point it's go to sleep. I didn't even want to shower, and I hated sleeping in my bed without taking a shower. I just couldn't move and neither could he, because he was already sleep.

I just laid there and thought about my life and how things had changed for me. My life was going so good. I wished I could bring Jaxon back to life and kill his ass again. I knew I couldn't blame him for the choice that I made, but he definitely played his part. I hated that Shay ever gave that nigga the time of day, because he didn't deserve her. She had such a kind, sweet heart. The only bad thing was that she loved hard. That's why I feel so bad about the shit that happened with Kam. I had no idea that they were together. I know that people were saying that he had a girl, but I didn't think it was Shay. I was just happy that she had someone to love her the way that she should be loved.

I thought that I would never get over Kamery, but Allyn changed that. I hadn't thought about him since the day I moved here. When I thought back on the shit that I was doing to get his attention, I was ashamed. There was no way that I would every do anything like that again.

My only dilemma now was the fact that Allyn's dad was forcing him to set Kam and Kaye up. One thing about Shay was that she knew when I was lying. I couldn't lie to her. She would read my ass, so I just hoped she didn't ask me shit about Allyn or his dad.

NUKE

Meanwhile...

I had been on a million dates, but for some reason, I was nervous as hell. Brittany and I had been talking on the phone and texting none stop since the day that we met. I had so many women in my life, and none had intrigued me the way that she has. I took her out the other day and found myself standing outside of the store just staring at her. She was perfect... not too dark and not too light. That ass... oh my god. I couldn't wait until I had it bent over. It was so round and plump. She had the most beautiful smile. Just thinking about her was giving a nigga butterflies.

"Nigga, what the fuck are you thinking about. Nigga, your dick is getting rock and shit. You can drop me at the crib if you're about to be in the car, jacking off and shit," Rue expressed. I couldn't do anything but laugh, because I hadn't realized that my dick was getting hard while thinking about her.

"Fuck you, nigga."

"Nah, nigga! Apparently, you need to fuck somebody, because you're over here getting a boner and shit. Maybe you need to go home and beat your meat or some shit. I don't want to be in the car with no nigga and his dick is just getting hard out of nowhere. That shit is not cool," Rue fussed.

"Nigga, my bad. I was thinking about Brittany. She's got a nigga's head all fucked up."

"Damn, nigga. Y'all have been talking for a minute. You got the pussy yet? What the fuck you waiting on?" Rue asked.

"Says the nigga that's been with his girl almost a year and still ain't got no pussy," I replied. If looks could kill, my ass would be dead. That nigga played no games when it came to Kamina. That nigga was so in love that it was funny. We had been friends since grade school, and I never saw him be with one woman.

"Don't worry about me and my baby. We're good the way that we are," he muttered. All I could do was laugh. This was one of times I wished Rell was here. He would diffidently be clowning this nigga. Rue used to be the biggest hoe in school, and now that nigga was practically married.

For the next few minutes, we sat in silence. We were sitting outside Justin's house, waiting to see what kind of action the nigga had. We had been there for the past hour, and there was no movement, other than him taking the garbage out. Just as I was about to pull off, a black Tahoe pulled up. The windows were tinted, so I couldn't see who was in it. After about ten minutes, the last person we expected got out the back of the truck. I really didn't know him. I had just seen pictures of him. I didn't worry about anything else at this point. I just pulled off. I had seen all that I needed to see. That confirmed everything that we thought. Now, all we needed to do was dead these niggas, but for now, I was about drop this nigga off so that I could get ready for my date.

I jumped on the highway and headed to Rue's house.

"Aye, nigga… can you stop at Dixie Queen so that I can get Kamina something to eat," Rue asked.

"Yeah, I can do that. I don't want her to kick your ass. We need to get these niggas, and get on with our life. They're slowing my money down, and that's a problem. I've got shit that I need to pay for like school.

After we went to Dixie Queen, and I dropped I'm off, I headed home so that I could jump in the shower. As soon as I got out the shower, I texted Brittany.

Me: Hey, pretty lady. I will be on the way in thirty minutes

Pretty Lady: Okay, call me when you're leaving your house, bucket head

I did reply. I just smiled and threw my phone on the bed before I walked to closet. I didn't really know what to put on, so I just grabbed a pair of white Balmain jeans, a white YSL shirt, and my white, French Blue Jordan 12's with my blue and white Givenchy Blazer. After getting dressed, I looked myself over in the mirror and headed out the door.

Me: On my way, Pretty Lady

Pretty Lady: Ok

I was feeling myself as I rode while listening to that new MoneyBagg and Yo Gotti. I rapped along with Gotti as he spit the last verse of Mitch as I pulled up to her house. I cut the radio down and jumped out before I headed to her front door. When I knocked, her mom came to the door. Damn, this old lady was fine ass fuck. The last time that I saw her, she was beaten up and had bruises all over her face and body. I guess he understood, because Brittany hadn't told me anything.

"Hey, Mrs. Glover," I said when she opened the door.

"Aren't you looking handsome today," Brittany's mother smiled.

"Brittany, Brian is here," she yelled.

Soon as she said that, her dad came in the living room where I was standing.

"What's good?" I asked, nodding my head toward him. He didn't reply. He just walked back into the kitchen.

"You guys have fun," her mother said as we walked to the door.

"Brian, make sure you take good care of her and have her home at a decent hour. We have church in the morning," she finished. I just nodded, because I couldn't speak. Brittany was coming down the stairs, and that alone had me lost for words. She was stunning, wearing a Red and Blue bandage dress and some red pumps.

"Do you hear me, son?" her mother said, pulling me from the daze that Brittany had me in.

"Yes, ma'am," I replied, giving her my attention.

When she made it down the stairs, I greeted her.

"You look stunning, Pretty Lady," I said, helping her down that last few stairs.

"Thanks... you don't look too bad yourself," she smiled. We

talked to her mother for a while longer and then headed out so that we wouldn't be late for our reservations. I was doing my best to keep my composure, but she was bringing the beast out of me with the way her ass was jiggling in that damn dress.

God, please give me the will power not to rip this dress off of her.

The rest of the night went great. I think this was the first time that I had been out with a female and didn't expect sex when it was all over.

NYLA

A few days later...

$\mathcal{I}$ would be so happy when this little girl got here, because she was killing me. I didn't have to go through all of this pain with SJ. My pregnancy was so easy, but this little lady was giving the blues. Shannon even had to get me a new car, because my stomach was too big to fit in my Porsche. Other than her giving me issues, life has been great for me.

I just finished my Masters in Human Resources Management. My marriage is great, and I'm finally having my daughter that I have always wanted. The only thing that I would change right now was my living arrangements. Like Shayla and Reagan, I was ready to be in my own house. I was too old to be living with anyone. Don't get me wrong. Kamin's house was nice, but I wanted to be at my own house.

Today, the girls and I were going to look at some houses and find Kamina a prom dress. I had been sitting in the tub for the past hour. As I said, this baby was killing me, and I knew that I am going to be doing a lot of walking. I wanted to make sure my body was relaxed.

"Baby, you still in the tub? They're all downstairs. You're the only one that is not ready. Get up and get dressed," Shannon said, walking over to the tub. He helped me out, and I headed to get dressed. When I came out of the bathroom, Shan and SJ were laying in the bed and looking at Paw Patrol.

"Baby, make sure you find something today. I want to be settled before the baby comes, and the way that you're walking, I think she will be here soon," Shan said.

"Okay, baby. I will try. Earlier, I was looking online. I saw one off of Forest Hill-Irene that I thought was really nice, and so did Shay and Reagan. I know that you didn't to be in Collierville. I don't want to go to Cordova. We need to be somewhere gated. I saw one behind Baptist that I want to go and look at as well," I told him as I slipped my wedding ring on.

"Okay, baby. That's cool. Just find something. I'm ready to walk around in draws and shit. Oh and I'm ready to see you cook in the little shorts that I like," he smiled. Shan couldn't have a conversation without saying something about sex. I didn't worry about replying. I just grabbed my purse, kissing him and SJ before walking out of the room.

"About time… with your slow ass," Reagan fussed, picking her purse up and walking to the door. I just laughed and walk out behind her. She was forever complaining when she is the queen of being late.

"Y'all want to go look at the ones behind Baptist first?" Shay asked. We all agreed before pulling off from the house.

"Can we stop and get Brittany? She needs to look for a dress, too," Kamina asked as we entered on the e-way.

"Sure," Reagan answered. I really liked Brittany. She was the sweetest little girl. She and Kamina reminded me so much of Shay and Reagan.

The ride to Brittany's house was quiet as we all were in our thoughts. I was just looking around at my girls. We have overcome so much. Most women would have given up a long time ago, but we all had made it through. We were rebuilding over lives day by day. As for Shay, I was just so happy that she was okay. I don't know what I would do if I lost my child. Don't get me wrong. For the first few weeks, Shay didn't talk to anyone… not even Kamery. It was like she was slowly getting back to herself, and I was so happy about that.

"After we all move, y'all needy to start looking for dresses," Shay insisted. I really had forgotten that she was getting married. All that shit that happened in Columbia threw me off.

"What color?" I questioned.

"Black. Y'all can choose what dresses you want. I hope I can find someone that can make them for me," Shay confessed.

"I can make them," Brittany replied.

"That's what I'm going to college for. I made this dress that I have on as well as the one that Mina has on," she disclosed.

"Well, why the hell are we wasting time looked for dresses. How about you and Reagan make the bridesmaid dresses," Shay recommended.

"Reagan, you like design too?" Brittany asked. Reagan was the best at design. I didn't know she had started working on her clothing line yet. She had been saying that she would start after she had Kamden.

He was four months now, so I didn't know what the holdup was. All of us were talented in something different. Shay was a math genius, and Allynna could cook her ass off. *Damn, I missed my girl*, I thought to myself. I made a mental note to ask Shan if they had heard anything else about her. She had been gone for almost four months now.

"Yes, girl. I have had a love for fashion since I was a baby. Shay, that's a good idea," Reagan confessed. By the time we got finished brainstorming ideas for dresses, we were pulling up at one of the houses near Baptist. The house wasn't my style, but it was really nice. We looked at like five houses in that area. By the time we were done in the area, I was hungry as shit.

"I'm hungry. Y'all want to go to Season 52, or Ruth Chris?" I asked. We all agreed on Season 52. As soon as we made it in the building, we all headed to the restroom so that we could wash our hands. When we walked in, there were two females already in there which was fine, but they both had their noses turned up, and it didn't sit well with me. Normally, I was the quiet one, but they were really pushing me. I was going to say something, but I brushed it off and went into the stall to use the restroom.

SHAYLA

*W*e were all in the restroom of Season 52, waiting on Nyla to come out the stall when these two female started to talk out loud like they wanted us to hear their conversation. I was cool until the pregnant one said my brother's name.

"Girl, Shan's ass been running my ass up the wall. I can't wait until I have our baby," the pregnant girl said.

"Girl, I want his boy, Kaye. That nigga so fine," the other girl said. I looked over at Reagan, and she was so unbothered. That the shit was funny. Clearly, the two chicks didn't know that we were the petty crew.

"I never understood how a bitch could be okay with being a side chick. How are you going to claim a nigga that you can't even go in public with? I guess when you have low self-esteem, you have to get in where you fit in… even if it is with a married man," Kamina said while laughing. The look on the girl's face was priceless.

"I know right, Mina. I know they be feeling all depressed when they find out the nigga ain't even claiming your baby. I guess it be like that when you're fucking the whole city," Brittany added. Neither of them said anything else. They just walked out the bathroom. We all just laugh and head to our table. That shit was so damn funny, but when I got to the house, I was going to have to have a talk with Shan, because this type of shit could not be happening. After we got to the table, we ordered our food and discussed the houses that we viewed today.

"I really liked the last one that we looked at, and I like that there is a guard at the front, and all the houses are gated," Reagan said, taking a sip from her drink.

"Yeah, I do, too. The neighborhood is centrally located, versus Collierville. That shit is far as hell when you think about it, and I really like the second house. I know Shan will like the guest house in the back. He can smoke in there because he definitely can't smoke in my house. He won't have my baby high," I fussed before we all laughed.

"Well, let's call Sylvia. We can have her to come up here so we can let her know we want the houses," Shay recommended. I called Sylvia, and she arrived shortly after, joining us for dinner. Since we were paying cash, the seller sold to us for less than the asking price. We were set up to sign the paperwork next week. After leaving there, we dropped Brittany off at Brands, and then headed to the house. I was extra excited to tell my baby that I found us a house. As soon as we pulled in the driveway and the door of the van open, I vomited everywhere.

"You okay, sis?" Mina asked, rubbing my back.

"Yes, I'm okay. I think the food just didn't agree with me," I said, walking in the house. I went straight to the shower. I felt so nasty.

"What's wrong, baby?" Kam said, walking in the bathroom.

"I'm good, baby. I think I just need to lay down. Bring KJ in here so that I can lay down for a minute."

"Nah, he just got up. Get you some rest, baby. He's in there with pops," Kam ordered. I just nodded and got in the shower. When I was done, I didn't worry about putting on clothes. I just got in the bed. I was feeling so bad that I didn't get a chance to tell him that I found us a house. Since he was gone, I just texted him.

Me: Baby, I forgot to tell you that I found a house. We sign the papers next week.

My Big Daddy: Great, baby! What's the address?

Me: 6070 Wild Oaks Drive. It's behind Baptist. The only thing it needs is paint

My Big Daddy: okay... call Sylvia and have her to meet me there at 3

Me: Ok, baby. Love u

My Big Daddy: Love u

I couldn't wait to be on own shit. I thought I was sleepy, but I wasn't, so I grabbed my laptop and started looking a furniture for the house. After about an hour of looking, I was missing Kam, so I called him.

"What's up, ma?" he answered.

"I miss you. Come and get me and KJ."

"Okay, go ahead and get dressed. I'm down the street," he said before ending the call. I jumped up and put on some clothes. I wanted to be comfortable, so I just put on a black and burgundy Gucci sweat suit with my velvet Jordan 11's. I washed my hair went I got in the shower, so I just pulled it up into a messy bun and found KJ something to put on. When I walked in the den, KJ and his grandad were watching TV.

"Hey, mommy's lil' man," I said, getting his attention. He just smiled and looked back at the TV.

"Hey, dad," I greeted Kamin.

"Hey, baby girl," he replied before focusing back on his phone.

"You ready to get dressed, mommy's baby?" I asked KJ. As soon as plucked him, he just started crying. Kamin had me so spoiled that it made no sense.

"Shayla, put him down. He's okay. Just let him stay here," Kamin insisted. I didn't even reply. I just put KJ back down and kissed him before going back to the room and getting my purse. I walked in the room and Kam called to tell me that he was outside. I stopped in the den to kiss my baby again and headed out the door. I don't know what I going to do when we moved. That little boy loved his grandpas... both of them. I never got to have time with my own baby because they always have him.

"Damn, baby. You're looking good. You sure you don't want to just go back in the house?" Kam questioned as I got in the truck.

"No, we have all night for that," I replied. He just smiled before kissing me and pulling off. Damn, I love this man.

KAMERY

I hoped this house was as bomb as my baby said that it was, because I was ready to roll. I was too fucking old to be living with my damn mama and daddy. I knew they didn't mind, but I did. I liked fucking my baby at random, so this was not working out for me. The ride to the house was quiet. I kept taking glances at my baby. She was so amazing. There was nothing that I would change about her. She was a great mother, and that alone made me happy. I knew so many females that didn't give a damn about their kids.

"What are you thinking about, baby?" Shay asked me as she rubbed her hand over mine.

"Nothing really… just life and how honored I am to have you in my life," I confessed.

"Not as honored as I am," she smiled. Her smile was so beautiful and warming. I couldn't wait until I made her Mrs. Mareno.

"So have you started looking for a dress?" I asked.

"Nope."

When we were pulling up at the house, I was amazed at how beautiful it was, and the neighborhood was great. I think I liked the security at the gate more than anything.

"How much is it, baby?" I asked. I really didn't care. I just wanted to know.

"It's 1.5 million. I know that's a lot, but I love it, baby. It's safe, and the one that Regan and Kaye are moving in is around the corner... so is the one that Shan is getting. I love it, baby," she pleaded.

"Baby, you don't have to beg me to buy you anything. You can get whatever your heart desires."

She didn't reply. She just blushed and got out of the car. I could tell by the smile on her face that this was the house for us. As we walked through the house, I just took it in. The house was nothing short of amazing. The thirteen foot ceiling and the white marble floors were what won me over.

"Hey, you guys, the owner is coming by. They said that they can bring the paperwork with them if y'all like the property," Sylvia, out real estate agent, said as she walking in the kitchen.

"Yes, that would be good. If my baby likes it, I love it," I expressed. I knew that this would make her happy, and that's all that I ever wanted to do. Sylvia walked out the house to call the owner as we walked the opposite way to check out the pool area.

"Baby, do you still have the guy's number that did the remodeling to the other house. I wonder if he can come and paint the walls for us. I wanted to move in ASAP... like tomorrow after I left the doctor. If I didn't have dinner with the girls today, I would start soon as we get the keys."

"What girls?" I asked.

"Aw shit! I forgot to tell you. Me and Reagan are meeting up Jazz later," she explained.

"And what you going to the doctor for," I asked. She had just gone to the doctor before we came back to Memphis, so I didn't see a reason that she should be going again.

"I've been having these headaches, and I just wanted to get it checked out," she lied. I knew her like I knew myself. I know when she was lying, and when she was telling the truth. Right now, she was lying. It was okay, though. I would find out, because whether she knew it or not, I was going to the doctor with her. I didn't worry about replying. I just looked the house over once more and waited on the owner with the paperwork.

I loved the pool area, so I decide that I would go out there since Shay was on the phone with Reagan. I didn't want to hear their conversation. As soon as I stepped out the door, my text notification went off.

Kaye Money: What you doing, nigga?

Me: Looking at this house

Kaye Money: we did that shit earlier. We're moving in next week

Me: Sounds good… we are too. Shay wants to do it this week, but I don't know. Some of the walls need to be painted

Kaye Money: That's what's up. Y'all come to the warehouse when y'all done. We got some shit that we need to handle.

Me: say no mo

He didn't reply back which I knew that he wouldn't do anyway. After about twenty minutes, Shay came and got me. We all met in the kitchen. We signed the paperwork, and the owner left.

"Baby, I'm so happy! I love this house," she said, walking toward me. When she made it over to me, she kissed me softly on the lips. That shit made my dick stand straight up.

"You better stop that shit before I have your ass bent over on this counter," I said in a joking tone, but she knew that I was dead serious. When the words left my mouth, my baby dropped down to her knees and took my full length in her mouth. That shit was amazing. I didn't want to toot my own horn, but your boy was packing, and my baby swallowed all of me. She was moving her tongue in a circular motion that was driving me fucking crazy. As she moved faster, her hand slowly rubbed my balls, and that shit had me ready to bust.

"Fuck, baby," I moaned. She had my toes curling.

"I'm about to nut, baby," I yelled, grabbing a hand full of her hair. It was like that was all the motivation that she needed, because she started moving faster. She was sucking my dick so good that my knees felt like they were about to give out.

When she was done, I took her to the back of the house where the master bedroom was located. Soon as the door closed, we got undressed. She laid on the floor with her legs wide open. I had the best view in the world right at this moment. My dick stood up harder than before. I dove head first into her pussy. I made sure that I licked every spot in-between her legs. Before I knew it, she was squirting all over my face. As we kissed, I slowly slid my dick in her, making sure she felt every stroke. I was hitting her lady button with every stroke. Just hearing how wet she was made me want to nut right then, but there was no way that I could get a nut without my baby getting a second one.

"Baby, can daddy nut all in that pussy," I moaned.

"Yes, daddy! Nut where ever you want," she damn near yelled.

"Why the fuck are you so wet, Shay? That's why a nigga's head is so fucked up," I expressed. That statement sent my baby over the top. I leaned back so that I could see her squirt all over me and the floor soon. As soon as she was done, I released in her. We both just laid on the floor for a minute so that we could catch our breath. We both got up and got dress before locking up and heading to the car.

SHAYLA

*A*fter mind blowing sex that we just had, all I wanted to do was go home and get in the bed. Kam always wore my little ass out. The fact that we lived in the house with some other people was what had been saving me. That was one thing that I was going to miss.

"Baby, what time do you have to meet Jazz," Kam asked as we pull out of the gate of our new home.

"At four, I think... why? What's up?" I questioned.

"Nothing. I was just asking. I think Reagan is at the warehouse already. Y'all can just drive our truck. I will ride with Kaye or Shan," he finished.

"Okay, that's cool."

The ride to their house was going to be long, so I pulled out my phone and opened the kindle apps. I had been reading this series for the past week, and I was ready to get done with it so that I could move on to another one.

Reading was my go to thing to do. After I lost my baby, all I did was read. Kam used to have to take my phone and hide just so that I wouldn't read all day. Every time I thought about my baby, I got sad all over again. I just wished that I could bring her back. Life would be so much better, but as my mother said, God makes everything happen for a reason. I have no idea what that reason is, and I don't plan on questioning God. Before I knew it, we were pulling up at the warehouse.

"You okay, baby?" Kam asked as he helped me out of the truck. I just nodded yes and grabbed my purse. I was nowhere near okay, but I didn't want him to worry about me, so a head nod would have to do for now.

When we walked in the warehouse, I spoke to everyone and went to the bathroom so that I could get myself together. After I was done I join everyone else.

"Okay, so now that everyone is here... We sat outside of Justin's house for I know three hours, and there was no action. Just as we were about to pull off, a black SUV pulled up and Angelo jumped out. The crazy part is that his son was with him. I could have sworn that y'all said that the nigga was not fucking with his daddy. They looked like a big happy family, from what I could see," Nuke explained.

At this point, my wheels were spinning. Allyn was one of the few people that knew that we were going to Columbia. Now that I thought about it, he was the only one outside of Nuke that knew we were leaving. I knew that Nuke wasn't the cause of the explosion, because Kam and Kaye were like big brothers to him, and I just knew he wouldn't do that to us. I sat on the desk as I thought on all of the things that had happened. We still hadn't figured out who did the incident at the club when Reagan and I were attacked. We all knew that it was Jamal's brother, but why did he do it, was the question. We still hadn't found out who did that. There were so many unsolved issues that didn't add up. I looked down at my phone and realized that it was twenty minutes until four.

"Reagan, you ready to get out of here so that we can go and meet Jazz?" I asked as I got down off the desk.

"Yeah, let's roll so we can see what we can get out of her. I know that if she knows anything, she will tell us," Reagan finished as we headed toward the door. Once we were outside the warehouse, the vomit that I had been holding back came up.

"So... when are you going to tell Kam?" Reagan asked as she got in the truck.

"Tell him what?" I asked with an attitude.

"Ummm, let's see ... that you're pregnant," she stated.

"What makes you say that?" I questioned as I started the truck.

"Don't worry about it," she fussed before cutting the radio up. We rode downtown in silence. I hated that she knew me so well. I didn't plan on telling anyone. I had done good hiding it for the past month, but all this vomiting that I had been doing was giving it away. The only person that knew was my mother, and she only knew because she was the one that told me that I was pregnant.

When we pulled up to Westy's, I shut the engine off and looked over at Rea. There was no way that I could lie to my best friend. She knew me too well.

"Okay, Rea... yes I'm pregnant," I confessed. She didn't reply. She just laughed and got out of the truck. I knew that she was going to go in on my ass later, so I just took the silence as a win. Soon as we were walking in Westy's, we found Jazmine sitting the corner.

"Why have you been crying?" Reagan asked as soon as we walked up to the table.

"Girl, all of this shit is just too much for me. His dad is running him crazy, so he is running me crazy. I love him, but it's draining me," Jasmine confessed.

I kind of felt bad for her. I think it was more so because she was dragged into all of this drama that was going on. It really had nothing to do with her, but like us, her man was involved, so that put her right in the middle. Shit was getting ugly and fast. The only plus was that she was still the same Jazz. She wore her emotions on her sleeve. On top of that, when it came to me and Reagan, she was an open book. After talking for a few hours and having a few drinks, she had told us everything that we needed to know about Angelo and his plot.

JEANO

Sorrento, Italy

I had been in Italy for the past week, and I still had no luck on finding Allynna. I had one lead, and that was a dead end. I still had her Kindle with me, and I was hoping that she would download something so I that I could trace it. I missed her so much that when I did find her, I was making her my wife. There was no way that I was letting her get away. I had been staying at a hotel that was near where her last download was done. I had been checking her Kindle every five minutes, hoping that she would just download anything. I just needed to find her. I was praying that she was okay. Nah, fuck that. I needed her to be okay. I was sitting on the balcony of my room, looking through the books that were on her Kindle like I did every day when my phone rang. I looked down to see my sister, Reagan, was calling.

"What's good, sis?" I answered.

"Nothing… just wanted to fill you in on what's going on," she said.

"Okay, cool. I was going to call y'all later to see what happened when y'all met with Jazmine."

"So check this… She said that Angelo is the reason for all of this, and he was forcing Allyn to set Kam and Kaye up. He wanted to knock them out so that Justin and his brother could run the whole south, and he could supply them.

I asked her if Allyn had talked to his sister. She said that Angelo was over the other day, and he said something about having Allynna, and that she was back home. She has to be there. Just keep looking for her, Jeano. Find her, and bring her home," Reagan finished. We talked for a little longer, and then ended the call. Just as I hung up the phone, I scrolled through her Kindle again, and she downloaded another book. I hurried and called Wizz to let him know to check and see if he could find the location. To my surprise, it was a coffee shop that wasn't far from my hotel. The only way that I knew was because I remembered her telling me that it was one of her favorite places and I went there to see if she had been there when I first made it Italy.

I was walking down the street, and something told me to look over. There you had it. Allynna was in the store, shopping without a care in the world. I stood there and watched for a minute just to see if anything was out of place. The only thing I noticed was the face that someone else other than me watching her… I mean, really watching her.

I walked into the store as if I was shopping, just to see if the guy would look my way. He couldn't look my way, because he was too busy looking at the lady that was at the counter. While they were talking, I slipped back into the dressing room area were Allynna had gone.

"So I guess I came all this way for nothing. No one is hiding you.

You're here on your own free will," I said, scaring the shit out of her. She didn't reply. She just stood there looking like she was seeing a ghost. After a minute, she just ran to me and hugged me tight.

"Baby you came for me. I knew you would," she cried.

"He has had me locked up in the house, all except one day a week. He had one of his guys following me everywhere I go to make sure I didn't call anyone. I got the message on my Kindle that was uploaded, but I had no way of replying. I'm so happy you came for me, Jeano. You have to call Kaye and tell him that Angelo is sending some guy to Kamin's house tomorrow. He knows that's where everyone is staying. He paid the guy at the gate to let his guys in. Call now. How are we going to get out of here without him seeing us?" she finished.

I just stood there for a minute to take in what she was saying, then made the call to Kaye. After that, I walked back out of the dressing area to see if anyone else was in the store other than us. Luckily, their stock room was attached to the dressing area. I came back from checking the stock room. I heard the guy ask, "You okay in there?" he questioned.

"Yeah, just trying these dresses on. I will be out in a minute," she replied. He walked back to the front with ease. After he was gone, I walked back into the room that she was in and grabbed her hand, giving her the most passionate kiss ever. I missed my baby so much. There was nothing that I wouldn't do for her. After I checked that the coast was clear, we slid to the back of the store. Just as we were about to walk out of the door, the guy walked up behind us.

"Where do you think you are going with her?"

"Home," she replied before I could get my words out. He reached for her, and I reached for my forty. Before he had a chance, he was dead. We headed out the door only to be stopped again. I guess there were more people watching than I thought.

"Give me the girl, and you walk, or I take the girl, and you die," someone said from behind us as we walked down the alley behind the store. I stood in place for a minute, deciding what I wanted to do. When I looked over at Allynna, she smirked, letting me know what the next move was. I handed her my gun and she turned towards the guy like she was about to walk to him.

PEW!

She sent a bullet through that nigga's dome. I thought she was about to turn back toward me, but she didn't. She walked closer to him and unloaded another round in his head. That shit turned me on like a motherfucker. I had never seen her like this. She jogged back over to me and we headed down the alley without a care in the world.

"Next stop is Angelo's bitch ass," she said, shocking the hell out of me. We stopped at the hotel so that I could check that I didn't leave anything personal, and then headed to Angelo's house. The ride to his house was long as fuck. My mind was wondering all over the place. I was doing my best to keep my manhood from rising, but for some reason, it kept standing at attention.

"You want me to take care of that for you daddy?" she asked as if we weren't in a damn taxi. Before I could object she had my pants unzipped, and her mouth was around my dick. I was in fucking heaven.

"Damn, baby. I miss how the inside of your mouth feels," I moaned. I guess she did miss a nigga, because she was sucking me up in a major way.

"Fuck, baby. I'm about to nut," I moaned. Seconds later I released my seeds down her throat. My baby cleaned my shit off with no questions asked. Once she sat up and adjusted herself, I gave her a big juicy kiss. I knew the driver's dick had to be rock hard by now, because my baby was making noises that I haven't ever heard.

She ran down to me how we were going to approach the house and get in. It was like she had it all mapped out in her head. The shit was genius. At that moment, I felt like the new age Bonnie and Clyde.

ANGELO

"What do you mean, you can't find her? This is your second fuck up. You have been doing this way too long to be fucking up like this. Find her, now," I screamed into the phone at one of my men. He was supposed to have an eye on my daughter. If she got to a phone, she would mess my whole plan up. She knew too much. I should have killed her at the fucking hospital, but I guess I have a soft spot for her. If she would have stuck to the plan in the beginning, we wouldn't be going through this, but what could I expect? She didn't have my blood running through her. The only child that had my blood running through them went through with the plan. Angela was my heart. When I had her set up that bastard, Kollin, she did it with no questions asked. If I could just get her to stop drinking so damn much... Ever since I killed her husband, she had been drinking nonstop.

I got up from my desk so that I could get another shot of vodka, and my office door flew open.

"Where the fuck have you been, Llynna. My men have been looking all over for you," I fussed. I was kind of relieved, because I thought someone had gotten her. I had so many enemies.

"Oh, I was tired of them watching me and of being here," she bluntly said. I didn't reply, because I didn't know how to. She hadn't ever talked to me that way. I just proceeded to pour myself a drink until I felt cold metal on my neck.

"You don't have time for that. We have somewhere to be," she demanded. I just sat the glass down and moved in the direction that she was ushering me in. I knew shit was about to take a turn for the worst when I saw that piece of shit that she called a boyfriend standing outside of my office.

"After all that I have done for you, you betray me once again, Allynna," I yelled. It was like I hadn't said anything to her. She didn't budge. After we were in my SUV, we pulled off from my house. When we pulled up to the airstrip, I just closed my eyes, because I knew what was about to happen. We boarded the plane, and to my surprise, one of my men was there waiting.

"Geo, I'm so happy to see you. Help me out of this damn thing that they have me tied in," I demanded. He just smiled and sat down like I hadn't said anything to him.

"Hello? Do you hear me? Get me untied, goddammit!" I commanded. They all just laughed and then carried on with their conversation like I hadn't said anything. I didn't worry about saying anything else. I just sat back and prayed my last prayer. I knew for a fact that this was my last day on earth.

SHANNON

The next night in Memphis...

$\mathcal{S}$ince we had been back in Memphis, we hadn't been out anywhere other than to shop for the houses. My baby did a great job of finding our house. It was nothing short of perfect. I couldn't wait until SJ saw it. Everyone had moved except us. Nyla wanted have all of the walls painted and dried before we moved in. SJ had asthma, and we didn't know how the smell of the paint would affect him. I was getting dress when Nyla walked in the room looking sexy as hell.

"Damn, baby. You sure you want to go out? We can just stay home if you want to," I said, licking my lips. I don't know what kind of dress she was wearing, but it was fitting her in all the right places. I walked over and kissed her on the neck. I hoped that she would let me slide in her before we headed out. We all were meeting up at Mynt Lounge.

"Stop, we need to get going. You know we're already late. She will be here when we get back. She's going to be hot and ready for you, so don't worry," Nyla smirked. I didn't worry about replying. I just grabbed her hand and headed out the door. My text notification went off soon as we got off the e-way.

Shay-Shay: *Where the hell y'all at? Everybody is here but y'all*

Me: *Pulling on the lot, damn*

Soon as we pulled up, I saw the whole crew standing outside, including Kamina and Brittany. This spot was packed. The owner of this joint is a guy that I went to school with named Brownlee. That nigga threw the hottest parties in the city. He brought the city out each and every time the doors opened. The food here was off the chain as well. We parked in the VIP section next to Kam's truck, and I hopped out so that I could help my baby get out.

"How y'all let Kaye and Raegan beat y'all here?" Kam asked as we walked up.

"Nigga, shut up. My wife is pregnant. She needs some extra time," I lied.

"I'm the reason we were late. I was trying to get some cutty."

They all laughed because they knew that I wasn't lying. As soon as we walked in the club, I laid eyes on the last person that I wanted to see. We all headed to the VIP area that was set up for us. I was just sitting back, chilling, when I saw Justin and the girl that used to be at Kesha's house walk in the door. I elbowed Kaye so that I could get his attention. When he followed my eyes, he got Kam and Shannon's attention. We got the women up and walked them toward the entrance of the club so that they could go outside to Kam's truck. Some shit was about to pop off, and there is no way that I would take a chance or either of them getting hurt.

Once they were in the car and safe, I headed back in the club. I made it just in time to see the Justin nigga walking toward the bathroom which was perfect. I spoke to my nigga, Brownlee, the owner of the club and had him to open the back door which was located near the bathroom. After he confirmed that it was already open, I headed in the direction of the bathroom. We have been cool since high school. I had him to unlock the back door so that we could head out soon as we snatch the nigga up. It was like everything was falling in line.

"Who do we have here," I said as I walked in the bathroom. That nigga damn near pissed all over his clothes. I couldn't help but to laugh. He was still silent. That alone led me to know that he knew today would be his last. Just as I was about to say something else, the bathroom door flew open. Kam and Kaye stepped in.

"Nigga, pull your pants up. We're ready to roll, and don't try any stupid shit. You know me very well, so know that I will dead your ass in this club," Kam said, walking toward the door. Justin did as he was told and pulled his pants up. When we made it to the truck, the nigga was crying like the little bitch that I knew he was.

"Look, man… I didn't want to do any of this. It was all my brother's idea. He was the one that wanted to link up with the nigga, Angelo, so that he could knock y'all out the box. Y'all have to believe me. We have been knowing each other since middle school. Y'all know I wouldn't do shit like this," Justin pleaded. As you know, all of the pleas went unheard. There was no way that this nigga would make it to see tomorrow. He had crossed the wrong group of niggas.

One thing that we were big on was loyalty. He was one of the most disloyal niggas that I knew. This nigga was ready to give his brother up without a second, though. Who does that? I would have been dead, because there was no way I would do any of my brothers like that.

He could say all day that he had nothing to do with the shit that had been going on, but we all knew that was a lie, especially since Jazmine spilled the beans on the whole operation that Angelo and Justin had going. I was amped that we finally got this nigga.

KAMERIN

*I*t was like God was working in our favor. We had ran smack into the one nigga that we were having a hard time finding. On our way to the warehouse, Rue called and said that they caught Justin's brother slipping. Now that we had them both, we could find out what the nigga's beef was with us.

The ride was quiet as hell. Everyone in the truck had on their game face except Shannon's silly ass. That nigga was never serious when he needed to be.

"What the fuck you smiling for, nigga. You over there looking like it's Christmas day," I teased Shannon.

"Fuck you, nigga," Shan laughed. I knew what he was smiling for, but I just wanted to fuck with him because I knew he would get mad.

When we pulled up to the warehouse, there was a truck that I had never seen, so that automatically put me on edge. Soon as Kam parked, we all jumped out and headed in. When we walked in the door, I stopped in my tracks. There had to be a God. There is no way that Angelo could be here right now.

"What do we have here?" I asked, walking toward the chairs that he was sitting in. He looked like he wanted to shit on himself.

"We got the fat bitch," Allynna said, walking from the office. All I could do was smile. I pulled my phone out to call Reagan.

"What's good, baby?" she answered.

"I need y'all here at the warehouse, pronto," I said before ending the call. I knew they were going to flip when they walked in here. We had Justin and his brother tied down. We shifted our attention to Allynna. I hugged her so tight. I was just happy that she was okay.

"Don't ever leave us again," Kam said to Allynna as he hugged her. She was balling at this point. I guess she missed us as much as we missed her.

We all had small talk as if Angelo, Justin, and his brother were not in the room. Like twenty minutes later, Reagan, Shay, and Nyla walked in with my dad and Uncle Ray right on their heels. They all stopped in their tracks when they saw Angelo sitting front and center. My dad just smiled as he walked toward him.

"I have been waiting for this moment," my dad said, pulling his phone out. He called someone and told them to pull up on us. That alone confused me, because the only people outside of the ones in this room that knew about this warehouse was our mothers, and I knew damn well he was not calling them up here.

"Angelo, I heard you were sending some nigga to my spot. That alone let me know that you had something to do with my plane. You couldn't have thought that I was going to let that ride. Better yet, I know you didn't think my kids would let it slide," Kamin damn near yelled. He was getting red in the face, and that was never a good thing. After about thirty minutes, the door opened and had all of our attention.

When I saw who walked in, I damn near died. There was no way that he could be here. I'd never met him, but I had seen enough pictures to know who he was.

"Allynna, this is your father... Kollin," my dad introduced them. Kollin hugged Allynna for what seemed like forever. When he let her go, he handed her a gun.

"Take care of that, baby girl," Kollin said to her. Without a second thought, she pulled the trigger, making him fly across the room. He brain spattered all over Justin and his brother. Allynna handed Kamin the gun and ran over to where Reagan, Shay, and Nyla was standing. She hugged each one of them as the tears flowed from her eyes.

The room was silent for a minute. We all just took the moment in.

"Give me that," Shay said, taking the gun out of Kam's hand.

"So all of this was your fault? You two are the reason that my baby is dead. She will never get to do any of the things that little girls do," she cried.

"I fucking hate you," she screamed as she beat Justin in the face with the butt of the gun.

"And to think... they fed you. They trusted you. You ....stupid bitch."

"I don't think I have seen her this angry, and honestly, I don't think I ever want to see it again. Each one of the women grabbed a gun and walked up next to Shay. Once they gave the go ahead, they let off round after round into the trio. If their asses weren't already dead from the blow that Shay was giving them, they damn sure were now. This shit was finally over. No, we can rest and live our lives in peace.

"Remind me not to cross y'all," Shan laughed.

"And you need to take care of the Kesha bitch before I do," Nyla said as she handed him the gun and wobbled toward the bathroom. We all busted out laughing.

"Well… looks like that we have one more on our hit list," I added. Shan should have taken care of her a long time ago. Reagan had already told me what happened when they went out for dinner, so I knew that she was going to say something at that point. I was just waiting and hoping that I was in the room when it happened.

ALLYN

The next day...

$\mathscr{I}$t had been a few days since I last heard from Angelo. Don't get it twisted. I wasn't complaining at all. My life was starting to feel normal for a moment, and I was enjoying it. Jazmine was flying back to Memphis for the weekend so that she could see her mother, so I decide to go with her so that I could see my sister. I hadn't talked to her since she went to Columbia, and that was not normal for us. I think that I had talked to Angela more than I had talked to Allynna. The last time that I talked to Angelo, she told me that she was in Italy visiting. That didn't make sense, because there wasn't any way that she would be going to visit his ass.

"Baby, you almost ready? The car will be here to get us in a minute," Jazz yelled from the living room.

"Yeah, baby. Just let me know when they get her," I replied. I had a lot that I needed to do when I got to Memphis, starting with talking to Kam to see how we can get Angelo and Justin out of the picture. I was tired of dealing with the both of them. I also needed to see about this cat that was trying to cop from me. The nigga said that Kaye referred him which was crazy to me. Kaye and Kam ran the game, so why would they send him to me.

"They're here, baby," Jazz said as she walked into my office. I shut my computer down and headed out behind her.

The flight was short as always. After we landed, I called Allynna so that I could see where she was.

"Hey, you forgot that you had a twin," she said.

""Never… I just thought you didn't want to talk to me. At least that's what Angelo told me," I replied. She was quiet which let me know that she had something to say.

"Since when do you believe anything that he says," she questioned.

"You are right. That motherfucker will lie just because. Have you talked to Angela lately?" I asked. Ever since Angela's husband was killed, she had been drinking a lot, and I was getting worried that it was weighing her down.

"No, I haven't. I need to call her and see how she is doing. Maybe we can convince her to move to Memphis," she added.

The phone was quiet for a minute.

"Spill it, Allynna," I said, getting irritated. There was something that she wanted to say. I hated when she did that.

"I killed Angelo," she muttered. I couldn't believe my ears. There was no way that my sister killed someone. She was the sweetest person ever.

"Where are you?" I questioned.

"I'm at home."

"Send me your address," was all I said before ending the call. I was stuck. I just couldn't believe my ears. I was free. At that moment, I could have cried tears of joy.

When we pulled up to the address that she sent me, Jazmine and I walked up to the door, hand in hand. After I rang the doorbell a few times, Jeano, Allynna's boyfriend, opened the door and let us in. I stopped in my tracks when I saw a man sitting on the couch that looked Identical to me. I was at a loss for words.

"Allyn, this is our father, Kollin," Allynna said as she walked over toward me. I couldn't move to save my life. I had dreamed of this day since I found out that Angelo was not my father.

"I thought he was dead," I said more to myself than to her.

"I did too... until the other day," she confessed.

"Where have you been?" I asked him. I needed answers. How could he just pop up out of nowhere? Now that I was looking at his face, I remembered him. He was the guy that used to come to my grandmother's house when we would go there to visit. I knew it was something about him.

"I have been around. I have watched you from afar," he answered. I just walked over and hugged him. I may not have had my mother, but now, I had my father. Life was finally coming together. Now, all I needed to do was find a way to plant some babies in Jazmine.

After I talked with him for a while, Jazz and I headed to our hotel. I also wanted to talk to her about moving to Memphis. I knew that she loved our house, but I was sure we could find one in Memphis that was even better.

KAMERY

A few days later...

$\mathcal{I}$ had been sitting on the bed, watching Shay get dressed for the past hour. I wanted to question her about why she had been so sick lately. I knew what was wrong. I just wanted to see how long it would take her to tell me. I guess I hadn't said anything, more so, because she was slowly getting back to the old her. I didn't want to do anything that would make her mad. I loved how happy she had been for the past few weeks.

"Hey, baby," she danced over to me. She was forever listening to Rihanna. This was her "getting ready" album. No matter where we were going, she had to listen to some sort of music while she got dress which was good for me. That's the way I determined her mood. I was dressed and ready to go, and she didn't even know it. I had even gotten KJ dressed.

"Hey, how much longer until you are ready?" I asked as I walked into the bathroom.

"You going to the doctor with me. I can drive myself, baby. I'm sure you have some stuff to handle with the guys," she mumbled.

"Nope… I'm with you all day, baby girl."

I knew that pissed her off, but I didn't really care. I just walked out of the bathroom and went to sit back on the bed. She thought she was going to get away. It wasn't happening. I guess she knew that, because she just cut the music back up and finished playing in her hair. It really didn't look like she was doing anything to me, but I was a man, so maybe I didn't understand. Once I saw her putting away all the stuff that she had scattered over the counter up, I left the room so that I could grab KJ. I just stood in the doorway of his room and watched him play with his toys. My little man was really growing up.

"K, what you doing in here," I asked, getting his attention. As soon as he laid eyes on me, he made his way over to where I was standing.

"Da-Da," he said, holding his hand out so that I could pick him up. He was all for "Da-Da" until he saw his mama coming down the hall. He damn near jumped out of my arm.

"Hey, mommy's baby. Daddy got you dressed and ready to go, I see," she laughed.

"Don't y'all look cute," she teased. I had KJ and I dressed alike in a black Nike fleece sweat suit and blue Handicap Foamposites. You know my lil' nigga had to be fly like his daddy. After she packed his bag, we headed out. I double checked all the doors and headed to the car. When we got in the car, I just sat there for a minute and admired my baby. She was glowing and looking beautiful as always. I loved the glow that she had when she was pregnant.

"What's wrong, baby," she asked as she adjusted herself in the truck.

"Nothing, baby... just admiring how perfect you are," I confessed. She was blushing as always. I love the way that her nose turned red when she blushed.

"You're so corny, bae," she giggled. The rest of the ride was all about KJ and whatever he was in the back seat saying. When we made it to the doctor's office, we signed in and waited for our name to be called. We made a little small talk about the family and having a cook out for Kamina's eighteenth birthday.

"Shay Bridges."

She was so into that damn phone that she didn't even hear her name being called.

"Bae, she's calling you," I said, pulling her from her phone.

"Aww, damn. I didn't hear her, baby," she said as she hurried and walked to the door. I grabbed KJ, and we headed back. After they weighed her and stuff, they placed us in a room.

"Baby, I've been meaning to tell you that you did a good job finding that house. I love it," I complimented her.

"Thanks, baby. I knew you would love it, baby," she confidently said.

"I want to have the wedding at Tower Center or Cadre," I added.

"I like Tower Center better. There is no parking downtown, baby. I don't want people to be late because they couldn't find a place to park," she confessed. I just nodded in agreement because she was right. I hadn't really thought about parking.

"Baby, how soon can we get married? I want you to be pregnant at the wedding," I confessed. I knew that she wanted to curse me out, but she didn't. She just smiled. Just as she was about to reply, the doctor walked in the room. That was my way of letting her know that I knew that she was pregnant.

"Good evening, Ms. Bridges and Mr. Moreno," the doctor greeted us.

"What's good, doc?" I replied. I was trying my best to stay calm, but I was super excited.

"Well, since you are here, that lets me know that you already know that you are pregnant. My question is, why did you wait so long to come?" the doctor asked.

"What do you mean 'waited so long'? How soon should I have come?" Shay questioned the doctor. I could see her getting mad, so I jumped in to calm her.

"What do you mean, doc'?" I asked.

"Based on the test that was ran, Shayla is almost five months pregnant. If you would like, I can do an ultrasound, and tell you the sex of the baby," the doctor said. Neither of us said anything. I guess we both were in deep thought. KJ was only seven months. That meant he would be just turning one when she had the baby.

"Are you sure I'm that far along?" Shay questioned.

"Yeah, but we can double check. Let's head to the ultrasound room and see."

We grabbed our things and followed the doctor into the room that was at the end of the hall. Once Shay was in the chair and laid back, the doctor put some gel stuff on her stomach. As soon as the little round thing touched her stomach, a loud heartbeat filled the room. KJ was just as excited as me.

"Okay, Ms. Bridges. It looks like I was correct. You are a week from five months, and you are having a baby girl," the doctor confirmed. At that moment, my baby broke down crying. When KJ noticed that she was crying, he climbed out my lap and over to his mom. He laid under her just like he used to do when she would cry at night after Kayleigh was killed.

"Baby, God gave us a baby girl to replace Kayleigh. Baby, we're going be okay. Now, Kayleigh can watch over her big brother and little sister," Shay cried. My baby was smiling so big. I don't think she had been this happy in a long time. This was all that I have ever wanted for her. Now, all I needed to do was make her my wife.

REAGAN

$\mathcal{N}$ow that all of the drama was over, my life to could go back to normal. Today, the girls and I were doing a spa day, and I was amped. It had been so long since we had been able to just chill and go as we please. I was in my closet, looking for something to wear when Kamerin walked in.

"Where are you about to go, baby?" he asked, grabbing my ass. I don't know why he was doing that shit. He knew that I had somewhere to be. I didn't have on anything but a thong. Before I knew it, his finger was slipping in my hot box. I let out a soft moan as he moved his finger in different directions. *Damn, I loved when he did that*, I thought to myself.

He picked me up as he sat on the chase that was in my closet. He slowly slid me down on his lap, and that shit sent me over the top. My shit was so wet.

"Fuck, baby! Your shit so warm and wet," Kaye moaned. He was kissing all over my upper body. That was making me wetter and wetter. One thing that I would say about the man was that when it come to the bedroom, he played no games. He had me running up the wall every chance that he got. I didn't care where we were. He was trying to get some.

"Baby, slow down," he moaned as I rode dick like I was in the lead at a rodeo. My baby was moaning my name so loud that I'm sure the neighbors could hear him. I was double sure that Kamden was awake by now.

"Shit, Rea. Baby, can I nut all in my pussy?" he begged.

"Yeah, daddy. Nut wherever you want to," I moaned. Once I said that, we both release at the same time. I grabbed my clothes and headed to jump in the shower. After I was dressed, I texted Shay to let her know that I was ready, and then headed downstairs. I scrolled through IG while I waited for her to pull up. I posted a quick selfie as well. Just as I was about to get up and go to the door, my DM notification went off. I didn't worry about checking it. I just threw my phone in my purse.

"Baby, I'm gone," I yelled to Kamerin and headed out the door. After he replied, I headed out the house to Shay's truck. Once I got in, I greeted Shay and Allynna, and we headed to the spa.

"Where are Jazz and Nyla?" I questioned.

"Jazz is driving, and Nyla didn't feel good," Shay replied as we merged on the e-way. The rest of the ride was quiet.

"So when are you due?" I asked, breaking the silence. I knew that she was pregnant for the past few months. I just didn't speak on it, because I knew that she would swear that she wasn't.

"I'm four and a half months," she confessed. I was lost. I didn't even know how to reply. There was no way that she didn't know that she was pregnant. I was going to question her, but I decided that I would do that another time. I just grabbed my phone and check my IG. The

DM that came through when I was at home was from this guy named Greg that I had use to like me in high school. I sat and debated on if I wanted to reply back. I scrolled down his pics, and I must say that dude was fine ass fuck. I decided to reply back, since it was harmless. Before I could put my phone in my purse, my notifications were going off again. Let me find out that this nigga was waiting on a reply from me. I really had forgotten that IG tells you when the message has been read.

Greg_Da_God: Damn, ma! You looking good. Let a nigga slide through

Me: I don't think that's a good idea. I'm married now, Greg.

Greg_Da_God: That's cool. I'm just trying to kick it. I ain't trying to take your nigga's place

Me: ummmmm

Greg_Da_God: So I'm gonna see you?

Me: I will let u know

"Bitch, who the fuck you back there messaging, because we know it ain't your husband," Shay questioned. I didn't reply, because I knew she is team, Kaye. I just smiled.

Greg_Da_God: Ok... well, my number 645-869-7489

Me: Ok, I will hit you up

Before I could delete the thread, Shay snatched my phone out of my hand.

"Let me see who this nigga is," Shay said, clicking on his profile.

"Damn, bitch! Greg's lil' ugly ass got fine, and look at that six pack... Good God!" Shay finished.

"Let me see," Allynna said, taking the phone from Shayla.

"Damn, he is fine. He got a twin?" she asked. We all busted out laughing because she knew damn well that she wasn't about to cheat. She would probably tell on her damn self. I think she was the most honest person that I knew.

"Fine as he is… I might," Llynna said, handing me my phone back. Once we pulled up to the spa, we jumped out in a rush so that we wouldn't be late. They spa charged twenty-five dollars if you were late. Lucky for us, Jazz had already checked us in.

"Hey, boo," I greeted Jazmine as we walked in the room where we would be getting our treatment.

"Hey love," she said, greeting us. In a way, I was happy that we were mending our relationship with Jazz, because I really missed her. When Shay was in Miami, she was all that I had. I just was so upset that she betrayed Shay. That didn't sit well with me. I wished she would have just told her from the beginning, and all of this would have been avoided, but all that really matter was the fact that we were getting back to the old us. That's all that I cared about.

~

A week later …

Greg and I had been texting back and forth for the past few days, and we were really vibing. He was a really cool dude. I couldn't believe I never gave him a chance. In high school, he was such and dork. There is no way that I would have been caught talking to someone like him. Honestly, I still could get caught, because my husband would definitely kill us both. I don't see any harm in talking to him. We were just cool. He knew that nothing else was happening. I already told the nigga how crazy my husband was, so I hoped that he didn't think I would jeopardize my life. He was cool, but that nigga couldn't afford my lifestyle. He had something going, but not enough for me.

I was getting ready to meet Shay at Designz and got a call from Greg. I damn near didn't answer. I had been talking to him on a little prepaid phone that I got at Kroger. It wasn't anything fancy. I just didn't want to take a chance at him saving my real number. I wanted to be able to cut him off when I got ready. If he had my real number, that meant that even if blocked him, he could still call. All he had to do was call from another number.

(901) 496- 8876: What's up, ma? Haven't heard from you all day. You must don't miss a nigga.

Me: Nah, I've been busy all day. What's up?

(901) 496- 8876: Nun... hoping that I will get to see you today

Me: I don't know. I will have to see what all I have to do today

(901) 496- 8876: Ok, make time for a nigga, Rea. I just wanna see you. My address is 3365 Camel Lane. I will be waiting

I didn't worry about replying. I just powered the phone off and put it in my purse. Shortly after, I pulled up at Designz. Fashion was my thing. I was in charge of all of the inventory. I had been putting off doing orders for the past week. I had been so focused on getting shit together for the boutique that I was getting ready to open. This had been my dream for so long, and now that it is all coming to life, it was unbelievable. Sometimes, I want to cry, thinking about how happy I was. I have it all... a great husband, the most handsome son in the world, and the greatest family ever.

After I was done with inventory, I powered the phone back on and texted Greg.

Me: Wyd

(901) 496- 8876: Nothing... waiting on you

Me: Ok... on my way

I knew that going to see him was not a good idea, but I am a grown woman. I knew how to control myself. I knew when it was time to go. I knew my limits. Luckily for me, he lived in Olive Branch, so I didn't have to worry about anyone seeing me. About thirty minutes later, I pulled up to his house. It was beautiful. Maybe I underestimated him. I sat in the car for a few minutes just to take a minute to think if this was a good idea. After a minute, I decide that it couldn't do any harm, so I got out the car and headed to his door. When I made it to the door, I took a deep breath and held my hand up to knock. Before I could knock, the door flew open.

"I thought you wouldn't come," he smiled.

"Well, I'm here. You going to let me in, or are you going to just stand here?" I asked. He smiled and stepped to the side to let me by. When I walked in his house, I was amazed at how beautiful it was. I guess that nigga was getting a little money.

"Want something to drink?" he asked as we walked through the huge house.

"Sure," I replied, following behind him. Once we made it to what looked to be the den. He walked over to the bar and poured us both a drink.

"You're looking good, ma," he complimented before passing me the drink that he had fixed for me.

"Thanks."

The drink was mixed just right. I wasn't a big drinker, so I was feeling the drink after a few sips. Before I knew it, he was all over me. Even though I knew it was wrong, I liked it, so I didn't put any effort in stopping him.

I let out a soft moan and that was all the confirmation that he needed to make his move. My mind was telling me that I needed to stop him and get the hell out of dodge, but my body was saying something different. I wanted this man in the worst way, and I had no idea why. That was part of the reason that I have been avoiding coming around him. He slipped his hand under my dress, and that was all that she wrote. He had me in la la land. I was feeling shit that I thought only Kamerin could make me feel. I was fighting the orgasm that I was about to have. I guess he noticed, because he stuck one finger in as I opened my legs wider so that he can have better access to my dripping honey pot.

"Damn! What you doing?" I moaned.

"Showing you how much I've been thinking about you. Can I taste that pussy?" he asked. As bad as I wanted to say no, my body was doing the talking for me right now. I nodded.

"I can't hear you, Reagan."

"Yes," I managed to moan. When his tongue touched me, I was ready to cum. His tongue was moving all over my honey pot. I mean...

he was changing paces like he knew just how I liked it. I was grabbing his head and apparently he liked it, because he started sucking on my clit like he was sucking a milkshake through a straw.

"Ummm, shit! I'm about to cum, Greg," I moaned.

"Cum for me, Reagan," he commented, and as if on cue, my honey spilled. He stood over me and just stared at me.

"Why are you looking at me like that?" I asked while smiling.

"Cam I feel you, Reagan. Baby, I have been waiting on his. Please, ma... just for a minute," he begged. I just nodded.

He dropped his pants, and I instantly regretted to say yes. This nigga's shit had to be abnormal. My husband was huge, but his shit was gigantic. I just closed my eyes so that I could brace myself for the pain that I was about to endure. I just watched as he slid a condom on. All I could think about is my husband, but I had gone too far to turn around now.

"Relax, ma. I got you," Greg coached. I did as I was instructed, and he slowly slid inside of me. It hurt so good. I know that sounds crazy, but I meant just that. It was painful, but it felt so good.

"Fuck, Reagan. Damn, you feel so good. Damn, girl! You might have a nigga stalking your ass."

That was it for me. I couldn't do this. If he was saying that shit, then I knew he means it. There was no way I was putting myself in that situation. This nigga might try and get crazy for real, and I couldn't lose my family for a five minute fuck.

"Stop, Greg. I can't do this," I confessed. He was looking at me crazy, but he got up. As soon as he was off of me, I jumped up and grabbed my purse. I was moving so fast that I knocked the vase over that was on the table. I didn't worry about looking back to see if it broke. I was trying to get as far away from that nigga as I could. He was going to get a bitch killed. This was some shit that I wouldn't dare tell anyone. I was happy that I didn't tell anyone that I was coming over here.

I powered off the phone that I was calling him on and headed to Kamin's house to see Mina and Brit off to prom. I just hoped that Kaye don't try and have sex before I could get home and shower. If he did, my ass was as good as dead. My son would have to live without his mother, because my husband would surely kill me.

KAMINA

*E*very high school student looked forward to prom night, and I was no different. It took so long to come that I just knew that it would never get here. There were so many reasons that I was waiting for this day. One reason was because it meant that I was one step closer to college. Secondly, it meant that I would be eighteen, and Rue could make me a woman. Since I was a little girl, I had prided myself on staying a virgin until I was grown. I saw so many of my friends lose their virginity to niggas that didn't give a damn about them. When Brittany and I were in the eighth grade, we made a pact that we wouldn't have sex until we were out of high school. Brittany and I had been friends since we were in the fifth grade at Bruce Elementary.

The thing that I loved about Rue was that he had never pressured me. I know that a man had his needs, but my baby put mine before his. I gained so much respect for him over the past year. He could've been one of those guys that messed with a lot of women, but he wasn't. My baby was all for me. In all of this time, he had not given me a reason not to trust him.

I was so excited that I could barely think. The only think that was missing was my mom. No matter how fucked up she treated me, I still longed for her. I wasn't tripping though, because I had Kam and Kaye's mother. She was all that I could ever ask for in a mother. Although she had only been in my life a short while, she treated me like she gave birth to me. Through it all, I still wished that my mom was here to see me off to prom, and to see me walk across the stage. Sometimes, I really missed her. Things had not always been bad for me and my mother, but once it got bad, it was *really* bad. I remember the day that she walked out of my life like it was yesterday...

"Kamina, eat all of your food, and I mean it. Don't make me say it again," she yelled. Seeing that she was my mother, she should know first-hand that I hated peas and carrots, but because it was one of her favorites, she felt like she had to cook it every other day.

"Mommy, it's nasty. I told you that I don't like them. They make me feel like I have to throw up," I cried. She didn't reply. She just turned her focus back to the newspaper that she was reading. I just sat at the table and whimpered. I knew she was not going to let me get up until I was done, so I just forced myself to eat them. As soon as I swallowed them, they came back up. I vomited all over the table and my mother.

"You stupid little bitch," my mother yelled, slapping me over and over again. She slapped me so many times that my face went numb.

"I want my daddy," I cried.

She was so evil and low down that she wouldn't allow me to see my father, because he didn't want to be with her. The last time that I saw my father, he came up to the school and ate lunch with me. When my mother found out, she flipped out. I used to hear her on the phone with her friends, saying that the only reason that she didn't get rid of me was because she knew that I would guarantee that she would be taken care of her for the rest of her life.

"You know what. I'm tired of your ugly ass. You're ugly just like your bitch ass daddy. He doesn't give a fuck about you or me. I don't see how your dumb ass doesn't see that. As a matter of fact, get your daddy loving ass out my house! Go and find your bitch ass daddy," she yelled.

I was only ten at the time. How was I going to find my father without calling him? She wouldn't allow me to have his number. There was no way that I was going to be able to call him and tell him that she had put me out.

I couldn't believe that she was really doing this. What type of mother put her ten-year-old daughter out in the middle of the night? I guess I wasn't moving fast enough, because she got up and dragged me out the front door. I didn't know what to do. I sat on the porch, crying for what seemed like forever. I say that because it was starting to become daylight by the time that I got up and decide to start walking. My dad live nowhere near us, so getting to his house would take me forever. I knew that she was not going to let me back in, so I just got up grabbed my Barbie suitcase and headed to my dad's house.

That was a day that I will never forget. Just thinking about it made me mad all over again. Now that I thought about it, I didn't miss her.

"Fuck her," I muttered to myself.

"Fuck who?" Shay asked as she curled my hair.

"No one," I lied. I knew that I couldn't tell her what happened with my mom, because she would tell my brothers, and I'm more than sure they would kill her, even though it was years ago.

"If you say so," Shay replied. I didn't say anything back. I just rolled my eyes. Shay had a way of reading people. The shit was crazy.

"So… are you excited about tonight," she asked as she pinned my hair up.

"Yes, I am. I just hope the night is perfect like I have been dreaming of," I confessed. I had been thinking about how things would play out for the past month. I hadn't even told him what I had planned. I wanted to surprise him. He didn't talk about sex with me. I think I had brought it up more times than he had.

"It will be just like you want it to be. Don't let me forget to give y'all the keys to your room before y'all leave," Shay said as she did the finishing touches on my hair.

"What's wrong, Brittany," I asked. She had been so quiet, and I had no idea why, but I was about to find out.

"Nothing," Brittany said in a low sad tone.

Before I knew it, I jumped up and went to get the one person that could get her ass in line.

"Where the hell do you think you're going," Reagan said, blocking the door.

"To get Nuke, since she wants to act like nothing is wrong," I fussed.

"No, we don't have to go and get him, because she's going to tell us what the hell is wrong," Nyla said, looking over at her. She had a river of tears flowing down her face. I hated seeing her this way.

"I just don't understand my parents. My mom is so dumb for my dad. He runs her life. They are not coming to see me off to prom. How could they be so mean and hateful? My dad hates Nuke so much that he can't love me. I'm their only child. How could they do this to me?" she cried. Seeing her so heartbroken was killing me. I almost wanted to tell Shan. I knew he would handle his ass. I grabbed my phone and called Shannon, telling him to meet me in the hallway. When I walked in the hallway, he was standing there and looking crazy.

"What's wrong, sis?" he asked.

"I need you to go get Brit's mother… just her mother… not her dad."

He just nodded and walked off. I walked back in the room and finished getting my makeup done. I was going to fix this and fast.

RUE

I had been sitting downstairs at Kamina's house for the past three hours, waiting for her to get dressed. Since it was almost time for us to go, Nuke and I decided that we would go out back and smoke before getting dressed so that our clothes wouldn't smell like smoke.

"I think I'm going to ask Brittany to move in with me. I think her pops still be on some fuck shit, and I'd hate to have to murk his old ass," Nuke said before pulling off of the blunt and passing it to me.

"Do what you've got to do to protect her. From what baby told me, that's something that she has never had," I confessed. Mina had told me some stories that made me want to go a murk the nigga myself, but it was not my place so I stood down.

"Say no more," he said, passing me the blunt back. After we were done smoking, we headed into the house to get dressed. Your boy was about to be fly ass fuck. I had a red and black Gucci blazer with some black Gucci slacks and red Louboutin's with the spikes. Y'all know I had to match my baby's fly. When we made it back in the living room, Shannon was walking in with Brittany's mother. That was really weird, because I remembered Nuke saying that they were not coming.

"Hey, Mrs. Glover. What are you doing here?" Nuke asked.

"This nice young man came to get me so that I can see my baby," she smiled. He was looking at her ass like she was crazy. It was because he knew better, but she was here, and that's all that mattered.

"You look so nice, Brian," Brittany's mother said before sitting down next to me.

"And you must be Kamina's date?" she asked. I just nodded and got up. A few minutes later, Reagan and Shay were coming down the stairs with Kamina and Brittany following. I was in a daze. My baby was looking so good. I don't think I had ever looked at her in this way. I had to adjust my dick because I knew if Shan saw how hard she was making my dick, he would cut all this shit short. I just laughed to myself.

"Mama," Brittany yelled. She was so happy. I think she was holding her tears back. I knew that her mom topped her night.

"How did you get here?" she questioned.

"That young man came and picked me up," she said, pointing to Shannon. I knew that Kamina had sent him, so all I did was smile. As long as my baby was happy, I was happy.

Nuke was lost for words just like I was. They both looked stunning. The way that dress was fitting Kamina, she'd better hope she would be a virgin when she got home tonight. I walked over to Mina so that I could help her the rest of the way down the stairs. Nuke did the same for Brittany.

We took pictures for what seemed like forever before heading out the door. Just as we were about to finally walk out, Nuke stopped and turned around to face Brittany's mother.

"She is moving in with me after tonight," was all he said before walking out the door. He didn't even wait on the damn lady to respond before walking out. I just laughed and followed behind him. When we made it to the car, we all just busted out laughing.

"Nuke, did you really just tell my mother that," Brittany asked while laughing.

"Yeah, and that's what it is. I don't have time for your punk ass daddy," Nuke said before snapping a selfie with Brittany and posting it on Instagram. At this point, he had proven that he was really about her.

The rest of the ride, we laughed, joked, and snapped pictures on Instagram.

When we pulled up, the driver opened the door so that we could get out. All eyes were on us as we exited the truck. My baby was looking so good. I was more than sure I was going to have to pop off on one of these young niggas.

The rest of the night was perfect. We danced and laughed all night. The only problem that we had was this young nigga that thought he was going to dance with Kamina. After they were tired of dancing, we headed out. It took a minute to get downtown to the hotel, so we all just made small talk.

KAMINA

"Go Brittany... you going to U of M with Kamina," Rue asked. I was getting pissed again, because she was sad. I wish I could just smack the shit out of her dad. How could you not want your child to be great? I think my dad and brother would kill me if I said that I was not going to college.

"Nah, I don't have to money to go," Brittany muttered.

"Yeah, she's going," I said without looking up from my phone. If I knew Rue, at this point, he was feeling bad because he didn't mean to make her cry. Brittany just laid her head on Nuke's shoulder, and started looking back at her phone. When we made it to the hotel, we got out and headed to our rooms. Luckily for us, our rooms were right next to each other. As soon as the door opened, I kicked my shoes off and walked to the balcony. The view was awesome. I could stay out here forever. I was happy, because for one night, I was just a normal teenager. I didn't have to feel like someone was trying to kill me or my family. Thinking of my family, I needed to let them know that we made it safe. I would have to text everyone I just sent a message to in our group text. Once they replied, I locked my screen.

"You okay, baby?" Rue asked as he pulled my shoes off before walking outside where I was.

"Yeah, I'm good. Just think about life and Brit. Her parents are so fucked up in the head, and it has her that way. I'm just happy that she met Nuke. He makes her so happy."

I had pulled all of the pins out of my hair that was now cascading down my back. I think this was the first time that Rue had seen my hair straight. I normally wore it in the natural state.

"Baby, I love you hair," he said as he wrapped his arms around my waist and softly kissed me on the neck. I let out a soft moan. Him kissing me like this felt so weird. Normally, all he did was kiss me on the forehead. I turned around so that I was facing him, and just like any other time, he kissed me on the forehead.

"Why do you always do that, Rue?" I asked with an attitude. I hated when he did that. It made me feel like he didn't really like me the way that he said he did, but today, we were going to find out how much he really loved me.

"Because, Kamina… I don't want you to feel like I'm trying to force you to do anything that you don't want to do," he confessed. I didn't say anything. I just walked back in the room. He sat in the chair for a minute. I knew he thought that he had ruined the night, but what he didn't know was that he had just gotten it started.

When he walked back in the room, I was on the bed, ass naked. He stood there in awe. I knew that he was not expecting this at all. He was trying his best not to look, but I had my legs wide open. His dick was rising by the second. I got up and walked over to him, unbuttoning my shirt and then his pants. His shit was looking like it was about to burst through his pants.

"Baby, what you doing?" he moaned as I slid his dick in my mouth. His dick was so long and fat. I didn't think it was this big. I really didn't care. I didn't know what I was doing. I just did what I had seen the woman in videos do, and apparently, I was doing a good job.

"Get up, baby. I'm about to nut," he moaned. I didn't move. I swallowed that shit like it was a slushy. When I was done, he laid me back so that he could get a good view of my honey pot. After I was comfortable, he stuck his head in between my legs and started sucking on my clit. I had been waiting for the moment for so long that I didn't know how to control myself. I was about to cum as soon as his tongue touched me, but I didn't want him to feel like I was inexperienced.

"Baby, oh my gosh! What are you doing?" I moaned. It felt like he was writing his name all over my pussy. There was no way that I was letting this man go.

"Baby, I'm about to cum," I yelled.

"Cum for daddy," he said without letting go of my clit. When I came, he stood up and continued to thumb my pussy until I came again.

"You sure you want to do this," he asked as he adjusted himself on top of me. I could feel the pressure of him against my opening. It was painful, and he wasn't even inside of me. I didn't answer him. I just nodded.

"Baby, I need to hear you," he demanded. My shit was so wet that I could feel my juices flowing down my ass.

"Yes, Rue. I want you," I said, pulling him closer so that I could kiss him. He kissed me as he slowly made his way inside of me. The shit was so painful that I wanted to tell him to stop, but we had gotten too far. He was moving in and out of me, making me wetter and wetter. After a while, it was starting to feel good. Once he was all the way inside of me, I could feel him hitting something. I just didn't know what it was, but he was making me feel the same way he did when he was eating me.

"Ummmm, baby! That feels so good," I moaned. I was doing my best to keep up, but he was wearing my ass out. I didn't know how much more I could take.

"Rue," I moaned his name. It was like that's what he wanted to hear, because before I knew it, I could feel his dick contracting inside of me. If I wasn't in love before, I definitely was now.

JAZMINE

For the first time in a long time, I was happy. I had my man and my girls. It had been a long road, but we were slowly getting back to how we were. I was so happy for Shay and Kam. I know that sounded crazy coming from me, but it was true. She deserved to be happy. I thought I missed having Reagan on my side even more. She was my rock, and I was happy that it was starting to be that way again.

"Jazz, guess who has been sliding through my DM," Reagan laughed.

"Who?" I replied. It was weird for her to be entertaining anyone other than Kaye. She was one of these people that despised cheating. I remembered in high school, she kissed another boy while she was dating this guy name, Chris. She broke up with the damn boy because she felt like she had cheated.

"Greg Mason?"

"You're talking about big glasses Greg that used to follow you around school?" I questioned. That boy was so crazy about Reagan that he used to follow her everywhere that she went. He even changed his schedule so that they could be in the same classes.

"What rock did he climb from under?"

"Girl, I don't know. He wants to meet for lunch. I'm thinking about going," she confessed.

"I don't think you should do that, Rea," Allynna added. I didn't say it, but I totally agreed with her.

"It's just lunch. Damn," Rea fibbed.

"That nigga ain't trying to eat no damn food. He was trying to eat your ass. You're going to get that man killed," Shay added.

She was crazy as hell if she thought that Kaye would not find out. He was going to kill both of their asses, and she knew that. Even I knew that Kaye's ass was crazy. I remembered when they first met, and she was working at his club. This dude was trying to holla at her, and Kaye damn near broke every bone in the man's body. Just imagine what he would do if he found out she was spending time with another man.

"I don't understand what the big deal is. How will he know y'all are going to snitch on me or something," Reagan questioned. She knew damn well we wouldn't snitch on her.

"No, that's not what we are saying. That man runs the streets of Memphis. I'm more than sure Greg knew that you are married and who you are married to. Kaye is all over your Instagram and Facebook. I think that nigga may be trying to plot something. What makes him just message you out of the blue like that. You need to be careful with that shit, Rea," I explained.

"True," Shay agreed. I guess she forgot what her man did for a living. Something about this was not sitting right with me, but it was not my business, so I'm just going to leave it alone. I just hope it doesn't backfire on her.

After we left the spa, I headed back to the hotel so that I could spend some time with my man. When I walked in, the room was dark as hell which was unusual, because it was in the middle of the day. I walked over to the window to open the blinds. When I did, Allyn was in the middle of the floor on one knee, and all of my girls were standing behind him. Tears were streaming down my face. It was so many of them that my vision was getting blurry.

"Baby, you have been nothing short of a blessing since you came in my life," he started.

"I knew the first day that I laid eyes on you that I wanted you to be my wife. You accepted me just the way that I am, and you never judged me. I don't want to live this thing called life without you. Just give me the chance to show you the life that a woman like you deserves," he finished. I couldn't speak. All I could do was nod. This could really be my life. I never thought that I would find someone for me. No matter how much I beat myself up for the bad decisions that I made in my life, he never judged me. He loved me, no matter what.

"Yes, baby. I will marry you. Besides... our baby needs both of its parents," I added. When I said that, he jumped up so fast and picked me up off of my feet that it scared me. I never thought that I could be this happy. I guess God didn't forget about me. All of my prayers and begging for forgiveness had worked. Life couldn't get any better for me.

After everyone left, we just sat on the bed and talked. I learned more about him in this one night than I had in the time that we had known each other. No matter how happy I was, there was no way that I could deny the fact that I could call my parents and tell them that soon,

I would be married. They were too wrapped up in their own drama to care anything about what is going on in my life.

"You okay, baby? What's wrong?" Allyn asked as he rubbed my stomach.

"Nothing that I have control of, baby. I was just thinking about my parents. I kind of miss them."

"Well, why don't you call them? You will never know how they feel if you don't ask," he replied. I just shook my head. He was forever trying to give me advice. I could honestly say that he had been right each time. He was the one that told me that Regan and Shay would come around.

"I will call tomorrow. I just want to enjoy the moment with you right now, baby."

"Well, I know what you can do right now. You can show daddy how much you love him," he said, grabbing his dick. That shit turned me on. Seeing his print through his boxers was one of most favorite things.

Before I had time to brace myself, he was kissing me all over my body. It was like my body was on fire. I couldn't control my breathing as if this was our first time. By the time he made it to my honey pot, I was dripping. I didn't think I had ever been this wet before.

"Damn. My lil' man got you dripping baby. If this is what it's going to be like, I'm going to keep you pregnant. We're going to have a football team around this motherfucker," he laughed. He sure had a way of fucking up my grove.

"Damn, do you always have to say something stupid," I fussed, punching him in the shoulder. I was getting mad, and I had no idea why. I got up so that I could put my clothes back on. Before I could stand back up, I felt his dick entering me. As bad as I wanted to push him off of me, I couldn't. It was like his dick was made just for me. His dick fit me perfectly.

"Shit," I moaned. He was giving me the business. I mean... he was hit my G spot back to back. It was driving me insane. I just didn't know how much more that I could take.

"Shit, ma. I'm about to nut," he yelled, gripping my waist tighter. He was pulling me closer each time that I was trying to get away. Yes, I was running from the dick.

"Nut all in this pussy, baby," I moaned as loud as I could. I'm sure whoever was in the next room had reported us by now, but I didn't care. All I cared about at this moment was feeling my soon to be husband inside of me.

He released his full load inside of me. It was so much that it was dripping all over the sheets. At the rate that we were going, we would be sleeping on a bare bed, because these sheets were ruined. We made love until till the sun came up. We both were too tired and worn out, so we just laid there.

"Baby, what do think about moving back here to Memphis," he inquired. I sat there for a minute. It was like he was reading my mind.

"What took you so long," was my reply. He just laughed and rolled over. Now, life was really coming together. I couldn't be happier.

KAMERIN

A few weeks later...

$\mathcal{S}$ince we had gotten rid of all off the drama, shit had been much better. Today was the day that we got approved for the finishing touches on our club that was burned down. We put a twist on it this time. It was a lounge in the daytime, and a strip club at night. That was Shay's idea, of course. I don't know what was up with her and her strip club, but for some reason she loved them. Just like the other one, we all played a part.

Reagan and I were at home getting ready so that we could meet everyone there. She was in the shower, taking her time as always. I was dressed for the most part. The only thing that I needed to do was put my shoes on. I knew that I smoked a lot of weed, but I could have sworn that I heard Rea's text notification going off somewhere in here. I just didn't see her phone.

"Damn... there goes that sound go again," I said out loud to myself. Now the problem with all of this was that Reagan had her phone in the bathroom with her. I knew that because she had Pandora on. I knew damn well she didn't have a second phone that I didn't know about it.

As I walked closer to the dresser, I could hear the ringing sound. I opened the small door in the middle of her dresser, and there you had it… a phone. When I pulled it out, it was ringing again.

"Who is this?" I answered. Whoever was calling hung up as soon as they heard my voice, so I called the number back.

"Damn, baby. I hung up. I thought that was your nigga that answered. I have been texting you all morning," the male voice on the other end confessed. I still didn't say anything. I just wanted to see if he was going to say anything else. Like a dummy, he did.

"He must be at home. You're not saying anything. I can't wait to see you later, baby. I keep telling you that he won't know the difference."

I didn't worry about replying. I heard all that I needed to hear. I just ended that call and called Wizz.

"What's good, Kaye Money?" he answered.

"I need you to tell me whose number this is. I just sent it to you. I need to know the address as well," I added.

"Say no more. I will send it right over," he said before ending the call. I locked the screen and put the phone back where I got it from before I walked down the stairs. It was best that I get as far away from her a possible right now, because if not, she would end up dead. I sat in my office for a minute so that I could get my thoughts together. At this point, I was ready to kill both of them.

I couldn't believe Reagan would do some shit like this. I know that I had not always been the best husband, but damn. For a change, I was doing right, and she was around here entertaining bum ass niggas and making me look like a fucking fool. She had me fucked up. I was not about to let this shit slide. I ran up the stairs two at a time. Just as I was walking in the room, she was walking from the dresser where that phone was hiding. I didn't worry about saying anything, because my actions were going to speak for me.

As soon as she walked toward me, I grabbed her by the neck.

"Bitch, I give you every fucking thing, and you played me. You got me out here looking stupid. I bet you thought I wasn't going to find out that you were entertaining another nigga. Well, guess what? I know everything, and because of you, today is this nigga's last day on earth. I will fucking kill you, Reagan, and you know firsthand that no one will ever find your fucking body... just like they will never find his. Play with me if you want to, and I will show you," I yelled before throwing her down to the floor. I didn't waste my time looking at her, because I knew that she would make me feel bad. I just grabbed my shit and walked out of the room. I needed to be far away for Reagan.

When I got in the car, I called my brother. He was the only one that understood the stupid side of me.

"Where you at?" I asked as soon as he answered the phone.

"Just pulled up to Brands," he replied.

"Okay, don't leave. I'm on my way."

The drive there was quick, since I was going ninety miles an hour getting there. If I didn't get there before Wizz sent me that info, shit was going to get bad. I pulled up and I jumped out. I walked into the store and headed straight for my brother's office. I didn't even take the time to speak to Brittany, or anyone else for that matter.

"Kam, I fucked up," I cried once I closed the door behind me. I knew that putting my hands on her was wrong, but I was so angry that I couldn't help myself.

"What did you do, Kamerin?" Kam questioned in a stern tone.

"I found out Rea has been talking to some nigga named Greg," I confessed.

"Okay... that not telling me what you did, Kaye."

"I choked her, Kam. I didn't even see if she was okay. How could I do something like that to my wife? She is never going to forgive me. What if she leaves and takes my baby? What am I going to do?"

For the first time in my life, I was crying like a little bitch. I couldn't remember the last time that I cried.

"Calm down. I'm going to have Shay go and check on her."

Before he could pull his phone out, Shay and Reagan were busting in the office.

"Kamerin, you have lost your damn mind, putting your hands on her. She is your wife. You are supposed to protect her, not hurt her. I'm not saying what she did was okay, but putting your hands on her only made it worst. Now, we have a fucking meeting in two hours. I expect to see y'all there... together. Kam... baby, let's go. I'm hungry," she yelled and walked out of the office with Kam in tow.

I couldn't wait to see that nigga later. He just left a nigga here. What if she killed my ass? Even though I wasn't the one that fucked up this time, I still was scared. As much as I wanted to say fuck her,

I couldn't. I think it was because I had fucked up more than enough times in the past, and she forgave a nigga with no questions asked. It wasn't like the nigga said that they fucked. He was just asking to see her. I was going to still make her think that I was mad just to get under her skin.

REAGAN

$\mathscr{I}$ knew that what I did was wrong, but that still didn't give him the right to put his hands on me. He has cheated enough times for the both of us, and I never put my hands on him. I remembered the first time that I caught him cheating.

Jazz and I were at Houston, grabbing us some lunch. We had just eaten, and were getting ready to pay our ticket so that we could leave. It was a few day after his birthday. I had bought him some Gucci cologne for his birthday. It was my favorite scent, so I knew the smell from anywhere. I looked up from my purse, and to my surprise, he was hugged up, kissing some ratchet bitch. That shit broke my heart. I was so in love with him that I believed him when he told me that he was using her for money. Now that I thought about it, he really plucked me. This nigga owned a club. What could she offer him other than some pussy? I believed that nigga. I forgave him without a second thought.

"I'm listening," I calmly said.

"What the fuck are you listening for? I don't have shit to say, but you, on the other hand, need to start explaining," he yelled.

"I'm sorry," I mumbled.

"So you really like this nigga? Do you want to be with him,

because if you do, all you have to do is tell me, Reagan. I will let you go. It may hurt, but I will let you go. I didn't want to force you to be married to me. I know I haven't been the best, but baby, I love you," I pleaded. I felt so bad because this was so out of character for me. This was not me at all. Now that I was thinking straight, I wanted to kill myself. I let a nigga that fucked my cousin in high school come in-between me and my husband.

"No, baby. I want you," I cried, walking toward him. The closer I got, the further back he moved. It was like he didn't want me to touch him, and that alone broke me down ever more.

"Maybe we just need some time apart, Rea. I want you to cherish this marriage that same way that I do. Since the day that we said I do, I haven't looked another woman's way. I have tunnel vision. All I see is you, baby," he said as he sat on the end of the desk.

"No, I can't live without you, baby. Please don't leave me, baby. I said that I'm sorry," I cried. I was balling like somebody died. I needed him to know how sorry I was.

I was wrong in so many ways. I could never tell him that I fucked Greg. I knew for sure that he would leave me. What was I thinking? Was it wrong that because I got caught that I wanted to end things with Greg? What if I wouldn't have gotten caught? How far would this thing have gone? I didn't even know what made me want to talk to him. Not that I was with Kaye for is money, but that nigga was a bum compared to my baby.

"Why, Reagan?" he asked.

"I found out about the girl... Asia. I thought you were still messing with her," I confessed. A look of sympathy covered his face.

"Baby that shit is old. I promise. I'm sorry that I hid it from you. Please, let's just move past this," he said. He walked toward me and covered my lips with his. As you know, at this point, juices were flowing. He slipped his hand down my shorts and slowly slid his finger across my clit. That shit sent chills through my body. It was like he knew my body so well he had me on the verge of an orgasm that damn fast. Just as I was about to cum, he pulled his hand out and kissed me before walking off.

"Fix yourself. I will be waiting for you in the car," he yelled over his shoulder.

I was lost for words. That nigga had just really played me. I should kill his ass, but I would take that because when I got home, I was going to suck his dick and stop right before he nutted. He knew that I have no problem playing this game with him.

I was just happy that we were able to get past this. Greg was not worth me losing my family, especially since our lives were back to normal. We had been through so much, so there was no way that I could let someone that meant nothing to me end us.

I adjusted my clothes, looked myself over in the mirror and headed to the car where my man was waiting. Apparently, he knew me well, because he was standing at the car with the door open, waiting for me.

"Payback is a bitch," I muttered before kissing his lips and getting in the car. He just laughed and closed the door before walking to the driver's side of the car. The ride to Designz was short and quiet. We both were in thought as we pulled in the parking lot.

"Look, baby... I'm sorry for all the fucked up things that I have done, but please don't let this happen again. Just know that his blood is on your hands," he explained. I really thought he would let him live, but I was wrong. I should have known better. There was no way that he would let him live, and I knew that.

Once I made it to the car, we had to get KJ and then head home. That was something that I definitely learned from. I love my family too much to be making dumb decisions.

JEANO

Graduation day...

$\mathcal{I}$ had been planning this day for a while. Today was going to be a good day all around. Today was the day that Kamina would be graduating high school, and the day that I planned to ask my baby Allynna to be my wife. After her being gone, I knew that I wouldn't be able to live without her, so I wanted to make sure that I made her mine. I would have never thought that I would have met the love of my life in the manner that I did. I guess you never knew what life would bring. So much had happened in this past year that I would have never thought I would be this happy.

After almost losing everyone that I loved, I decided that it was time that I made some changes in my life. I'd be starting with marrying Allynna.

"Baby, are you almost ready," I yelled up the stairs to Allynna. Just like any other woman, she was taking all day to get dressed like we didn't have anywhere to be.

"Yeah, I'm done... just grabbing my purse, and then I'm heading down," she yelled back.

At that moment, I remembered that I needed to get Kamina and Brittany's gift. I knew that she would be another ten minutes, so I took that time to go to my office and grab their gifts. Since tomorrow was Llynna's birthday, we all decided that the graduation party would double as a birthday day party for Allynna. She had no idea. I'm sure she thought that we forgot with all of the shit that had been going on, but I would never forget such an important day.

When I was young, I never had anyone to acknowledge my birthday, and I said that when I got a family, I would make sure that theirs was special, no matter what. Just as I was walking out of my office, my baby was coming down the stair, looking stunning as always. The way that dress was fitting her had my dick ready to burst out my pants.

"Baby, why are you looking at me like that?" she questioned.

"I'm sorry, baby. It's just that you look so amazing," I confessed. She was looking so good in that damn dress that I wanted to peel it off, but that would have to wait until later. We needed to get going before we were late.

After we locked the house up, we headed to the car and made our way to Kamina's graduation. Soon as we pulled up, I got irritated at how many people were walking around. I was just happy that Shay already had a section blocked off for us. We walked in just in time, because they were getting ready to close the doors so that the graduates could march in. Soon as we sat down, all of my attention went to Rue. That little nigga was looking like a proud father or something.

"Damn, nigga! You're more excited than Kamin," I teased.

"I am. My baby is about walk across the stage," he announced. I don't think I had ever seen him so happy about something that didn't involve money. When he first started messing with Kamina, I was kind of pissed. I guess that was more so because I felt like one of my niggas was trying to fuck my lil' sister. Then, I thought about the fact that Rue knew that we would body his ass if he hurt her.

I think the only one that still hadn't gotten used to it was Shannon. That nigga got mad every time he saw them together. The shit would be so funny. A few minutes later, the graduates started marching in. I was so happy when I saw Kamina and Brittany walking up to sit on the stage. After hearing the speakers, and them calling nearly 500 names, graduation was over, and it was almost time for the big show. We all stood outside in the lobby and waited for Kamina to come out.

"There she go, y'all," Rue yelled over all of the people that were talking. Apparently, he was loud because she was able to hear him, and her head turned toward where we all were standing. Just as she was walking up, I grabbed my nephew from Reagan so that she could hug Kamina. After she hugged everyone, she walked over to me.

"Jeano Beano," she teased. That was a name that she and Brittany came up with. If she wasn't my little sister, there is no way that she would get away with calling me that bullshit. I handed Kamden to his dad and extended my arms to hug her. Just as I was wrapping my arms around her, my eye landed on Brittany and Nuke. Brittany was crying. I hugged Kamina and then walked over to where they were standing. Apparently, the whole family noticed and followed behind me.

"What's wrong? " I asked once I made to where they were

standing.

"Her family didn't come," Nuke confessed. That shit killed me. This was something that no child should have to deal with. This was one of the most important days in a child's life. Before I had a chance to say anything thing, Allynna grabbed her and hugged her. The hug was so tight that I didn't think that girl could breathe.

"It's okay, Brit," Allynna said, hugging her. I guess she felt the same pain before. She told me a while back that Angelo did come to their graduation when they graduated high school.

"I just don't understand. One day was all that I ask for that's it. You would think that she would be proud that their only child graduated at the top of her class. I made in through high school with no kids. I managed to make all A's while working a full-time job so that I could help them on bills. They always play this role in front of people like they really care about me. All they care about is themselves," she cried.

"All I wanted was one day," she repeated. You could see that hurt in her eyes, and that alone was fucking me up, because she was always so happy. I couldn't understand why her parents missed out on this day, especially since Nuke told me that they seemed to like that we were all about Brittany. Maybe it's like she said... just a front.

Once Brittany was calm, we all headed to Kamin's house for the party. I was getting more and more nervous by the minute. I knew that she would say yes, but there is a chance that she would say no.

"You okay, Jeano?" Kam asked as he sat next to me.

"Yes, I'm good... just afraid that she will say no, and I don't think that I will be able to take that," I mumbled.

"How likely is that to happen? That girl loves your shitty ass draws," Kam joked. I knew that she loved me, but I still just didn't know.

"I think I'm going to wait until another time. Maybe I need to do it when we are alone, so if she says no, I won't be embarrassed," I whined. I knew that I sounded like a little bitch, but that was just how I feel at the moment.

"What y'all niggas out here talking about?" Shan asked as he walked out the door.

"This nigga over here is acting like a lil' bitch, talking about he's going to wait and propose to Allynna when they're alone, so if she says no, he won't fell embarrassed," Kam snitched. I couldn't believe this nigga was telling on me like we were kids or some shit. I was a grown ass man. I was just happy that Kamin was not out her, because I knew that he would be all in my shit.

"Nigga, if you don't go on with bitch shit and make that damn girl your wife before some other nigga does it. That's why my ass married Nyla, quick. My mama told me that if I didn't marry her, some other nigga was going to do it, and there was no way that I could take that chance," Shan explained.

"That would be one dead nigga," I laughed. I hated to admit it, but what he was saying was true. I couldn't count how many times she had shown me a DM from thirsty ass niggas. I needed to be a man and give my baby my last name.

"Whatever, nigga. It's going to be another nigga sliding all in her pussy. She's going to be sucking that nigga's dick and licking his balls. Then, he's going to put plenty babies in her, and you ain't going to be able to do shit but watch from the sideline," Kam teased. That was enough for me. I was about to do this shit right now. Shit, I may take her ass right to the damn courthouse in the morning. I couldn't let her get away.

ALLYNNA

I was so happy with my life. Now that I didn't have Angelo to worry about, I felt so much better. All I ever wanted was to be happy. Now that I had my biological father, I felt complete. I just wished I had my mother here with me. I knew that she would have loved Jeano just as much as I did.

I had been sitting in one of the guest rooms for the past twenty minutes, just thinking about my life and how things seem to happen when you least expected. Seeing Brittany so torn up about her parents not coming to her graduation really brought back some memories.

The day before I graduated from high school I had gotten in trouble, because I didn't do my chores. So my punishment was him not coming to my graduation. Allyn didn't care either way, but I did I think it was more so because I didn't have friends like he did. He had a friend, and he was close to their families. I didn't have that. Actually, I didn't have any friends at all… not because I didn't want to. It was because I wasn't allowed to. Angelo didn't allow me to deal with anyone outside of school. I was just happy that Brittany had a friend with such a good family to fall back on. One thing that I would say is that if they considered you family, they treated you as just that. Since I had been in here a while, I decided that I would go in the back yard with everyone else.

"I was looking for you," Shay said, walking toward me.

"Aww, girl. I had to get myself together. Seeing Brittany cry today it took me to a place in my life that I never wanted to go back to," I replied as we walked to the back yard.

"Where is everybody?" I asked. There was no one in the house, and that was weird, since there were so many people here.

When we made it to the back yard, I was stuck in place. I couldn't talk. I couldn't move. I couldn't do anything. I didn't know how many other ways to say how I was feeling at that very moment.

"Baby, I know that you have been through so much. I also know that I don't want you to have to go through anything else alone. I want to wake up with you each and every day. I wake up every day, thanking God for placing you in my life. I'm not perfect, but I can do my best to be for you, baby," he said, down on one knee. I couldn't believe my eyes. I was standing there, crying… not able to speak. I just nodded my head. When I looked down at the rock that was in his hand, I got the courage to say what I needed.

"Hell yes, baby. I will marry you!" I yelled, snatching the ring from the box and slipping it on my finger. This had to be the best birthday ever. I didn't know how to act. I was about to get married. Yassssss, honey! I was so busy looking at this beautiful rock that my soon to be husband just gave me.

"I love you so much, Jeano. I can't wait to be your wife," I said, kissing him. He picked me up and spun me around. At this moment, all I wanted to do was go home and fuck my man, but that could wait.

I just wanted to enjoy my family and friends. This was something that I had never had, and I wanted to have this forever.

"Okay... now that we have that out the way, can we eat?" Nyla asked, making us all laugh. Even though she was almost nine months pregnant, you would have never known that she ate so much. She was hungry all day, every day, but she wasn't over 150 pounds.

"Well, y'all heard my wife. Let's eat," Shan announced. Everyone made their way in the house, except me. I just wanted to take in the moment. I would have never imaged that this would be happening. I never thought that I would find real love, and that someone would put me first. Who would know that being forced to be married to someone would lead you to find that love of your life? I didn't see how people stayed in an arranged marriage for so long. I couldn't see myself being with someone that I really didn't love for the rest of my life. I guess that's why my mother hated being with Angelo so much. I remember when she used to cry at night and say that she hated that she married him.

I think the person that I felt bad for the most was Angela. She wanted Angelo to accept her so bad that she allowed him to kill the only man that she had ever loved. I was so happy that my aunt told me the truth about Angelo. I would have been just like Angela.

"Hey, baby girl. You okay?" Kollin asked as he walked outside and sat next to me on the bench.

"Yeah, I'm good... just taking it all in."

"I just want to come out here and tell you that I am sorry. I could have killed him a long time ago, but I didn't want you to hate me. If I would have known what I know now, I would have. I know I have been gone most of your life, but I want the chance to make up for that. I loved your mother with everything in me. If I could have given my life for hers, I would have. She was the most amazing woman that I have ever meet. You remind me of her. You are all that I have that links me to her. I want to be the father that I should have been a long time ago," he finished.

"I forgive you. I know that my mother loved you. I know that if she was here, she would be so happy that you are in my life," I cried. We hugged for what seemed like forever. This was what I needed. I needed love. I was getting just that.

"Hey, baby. Here is your plate," Jeano said, forcing me and my dad to end our hug.

"Thanks, baby," I said, taking the plate from his hand. As I sat there eating, I just looked around at all of the people that I was blessed to have in my life. Two years ago, I wouldn't have ever thought that these people would love me the way that they do, especially Kamerin and Reagan. I caused so much drama in their lives, and they forgave me for all of it. I was so thankful.

I had to say that this day had been awesome. I was so happy with my life. This was the start of something great. After we were done eating, all of the women headed outside on the patio with the kids.

"I'm just so happy to have you guys. I don't think I would have made it through without you all having my back," I confessed.

"Well, I'm just happy that we all could come together as a family. No one would have thought that we would all be one family. Love is a powerful thing," Shay said, finishing off her cake.

"Girl, I remember that I was ready to kill you a year ago. If someone would have told me that you would end up being my sister in law, I would have beat their ass as well. All in all, I'm happy that I have each one of you in my life," Reagan added. We all just laughed. That damn girl didn't care what she said.

For the rest of the night, we just sat outside, laughed and talked. Before we knew it, the kids had played themselves to sleep. We all gathered our things and headed home.

SHALYA

4 months later...

"*B*aby, are you dressed?" Kamery yelled up the stairs. I didn't reply. I just rolled my eyes and kept curling my hair. He was forever rushing me.

"Damn, Shay. I know your ass hears me," he yelled again, but this time, I could hear him coming up the stairs. When I heard him getting closer, I cut my Pandora up a little louder so that I could pretend that I didn't hear him.

"Baby, I know you heard me talking to you. That damn phone ain't that loud, Shayla. The guest are starting to arrive, and you're in here, taking your damn time getting ready," Kam fussed. I just rolled my eyes. He acted like my ass wasn't eight months pregnant.

"Damn, I'm going as fast as I can. You act like I didn't get you and KJ ready first. It never fails. You always want to rush me after you're done," I fussed back at him. He had me fucked up, thinking that he was going to rush me to get ready and have me around here looking a hot fucking mess. He didn't reply. He just walked out of the room. I didn't care about him being mad. I just cut my music back up. After I was done curling my hair, I grabbed my clothes so that I could get dressed. I was keeping it simple today. I was wearing some Tru Religion jeans with a shirt that I had custom made just for today, and just like Kam and KJ, I slipped on my velvet Jordan 11's. I gave myself one more look over in the mirror and headed downstairs.

"About damn time," my husband said as he walked past me holding a bucket of ice. Yes, I did say my husband. We decided that we would just elope and have a wedding at another time, especially since I was pregnant. There was no way that I was going to be trying to plan a damn wedding. I thought that the family would have been mad, since we didn't take the time to have a real wedding.

"Shut up, and give me a kiss," I demanded as I walked in the kitchen behind him. He just smiled and turned around to kiss me. It was so passionate that it sent a chill through my body.

"Baby, can you go and put the cover over the pool. I don't need anybody's kids falling in," he ordered. I just shook my head and headed to the backyard so that I could do what I was told. Luckily I made it in time, because one of his worker's son was about to try and get in.

"Come on, lil' man," I said, grabbing him back before he made it to the edge.

"Whose damn child is this... because his ass doesn't need anything to eat. He is heavy as hell," I yelled across the yard, making everybody laugh.

"My bad, boss lady. That's my son," Dre, one of the guys that do security at the club, said as he grabbed his son from my hands.

After I handed him his child, I walked over to the wall to hit the button so that the pool would be covered. When I was done, I headed back in the house so that I could help with all of the last minute stuff. When I walked in my kitchen, Reagan was cutting up some fruit, so I grabbed a knife and joined her.

Just looking at Reagan made me so proud. She had made it through so much. Who would have thought in a year's time that she would be so happy and full of life after nearly being killed three times? I guess it was like they say… you've got to go through something to get somewhere.

"We should have done this shit yesterday. Hell, I want to sit back and chill like everyone else," Reagan fussed. Just as I was about to reply, Nyla walked in carrying my niece, Shanna. She was the cutest little girl that I had ever laid eyes on, outside of my Kayleigh. Nyla had just given birth to her a month and a half ago. She was a spitting image of SJ. The only difference was that she had my eyes. Both Shan and Nyla were doing very well. Shannon recently opened a tattoo shop, and it was doing really well. Nyla had just landed a great job as head of HR for FedEx. I was so happy for them all around.

"Hey, sis pooh. Hey, my teetee boo."

"Damn, what about me," Shannon whined as he walked toward me with SJ following behind.

"Hey, Shanny Pooh," I laughed as he walked in the kitchen.

"Don't be calling me that shit in front of all these folks," Shan fussed.

"Boy, please! Ain't nobody in this kitchen but family," Rea added. We all just busted out laughing. I don't know why that nigga hated to hear us call him that, but he did. He would blow a fucking gasket if we fucked up and called him that shit in public. He didn't reply. He just grabbed Shanna and headed outside with the rest of the men.

"So Nyla… how has the new job been going, boo?" I questioned. She held up one finger as she took a drink of Crown Royal.

"Girl, good. Some of those old ass women be pissing me off, but other than that, it's good. I really like it. I just don't like being away from my kids and husband," she confessed. I could tell by the look in her eye that she wouldn't be at that job long. She was so used to being home.

"Hey, y'all," Kamina damn near yelled as she walked in the kitchen with Rue in tow.

"Hey, loud mouth," I said, laughing. She just rolled her eyes as Rue walked over and hugged all of us before walking to the back of the house to where the bathrooms were.

Rue and Kamina were in a league of their own, for them to be so young. Since she graduated high school, she had started her own clothing line, and was now a freshman at the University of Memphis. I couldn't believe that her dad and brother let her move out, but they did. They bought a house not far from us. I would have never thought that their relationship would have made it this far, but from the looks of it, they were going places.

Soon as he was clear of the kitchen Reagan dove head first into asking the damn girl a million questions. She was asking them so fast that Kamina didn't have a chance to answer them all. After a minute, we all just walked off to go and see who was ringing the doorbell.

"I know damn well y'all bitches did not just walk out on me," Reagan yelled as she walked in the living room where we were all standing and greeting Jeano and Allynna.

"Girl, if you get any damn bigger, you're going to bust," Kamina joked. She wasn't lying, though. Allynna was only six months, but if you saw her, you would think that she passed her due date. I'm willing to bet that she was having twins. Neither of them wanted to admit it, though. I guess they were in denial. Every time we would bring it up, Jeano would say that he had too much going on for them to have twins. I just needed him to understand that life didn't happen that way. He couldn't choose what he wanted. God blessed you how he saw fit. I guess with Allynna and Allyn inheriting all of Angelo's business, and him owning one of the biggest security companies in Memphis, he didn't think that he could deal with the fact that he would be having two kids instead of one. On top of all of that, they were getting ready to get married.

"Girl, I feel like I'm about to bust," Allynna whined. It was so funny seeing her like this, because she made fun of me the whole time that I was pregnant.

After everyone was here, we all headed to the backyard so that we could get the party started. KJ was so happy and having so much fun that he didn't even have time to eat. I finally was able to get him to sit down long enough so that he could have a slice of pizza. I had to bribe him by telling him that I would let him open his gifts. Once we were done with that, I was finally able to sit down and just take in the scenery in front of me. I had my whole family here. Just seeing everyone happy and getting along was making me emotional.

I guess it was true with what they say. God placed people in your life for a reason, whether it was good or bad. I remembered my grandmother used to tell me that you had to appreciate the people in your life, and to always make them aware of how much they mean to you. We all came from different walks of life, but we were all walking in the same direction… toward greatness.

THE END

Looking for a publishing home?

Royalty Publishing House, Where the Royals reside, is accepting submissions for writers in the urban fiction genre. If you're interested, submit the first 3-4 chapters with your synopsis to submissions@royaltypublishinghouse.com.

Check out our website for more information: www.royaltypublishinghouse.com.

Text ROYALTY to 42828 to join our mailing list!

To submit a manuscript for our review, email us at
submissions@royaltypublishinghouse.com

Text RPHCHRISTIAN to 22828 for our
CHRISTIAN ROMANCE novels!

Text RPHROMANCE to 22828 for our
INTERRACIAL ROMANCE novels!

Do You Like CELEBRITY GOSSIP?

Check Out QUEEN DYNASTY!
Visit Our Site: www.thequeendynasty.com

Get LiT!

Download the LiTeReader app today and enjoy exclusive content, free books, and more

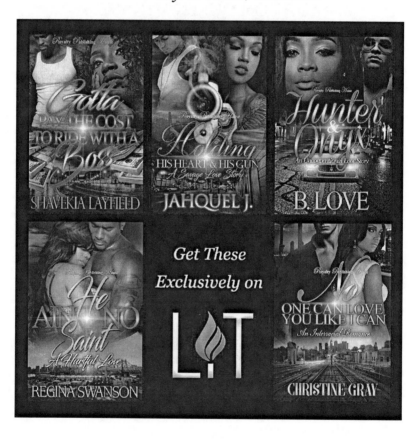

CPSIA information can be obtained
at www.ICGtesting.com
Printed in the USA
LVOW10s2029050217
523261LV00016B/1004/P

9 781542 657358